ALL THAT WE CARRY

STORIES ACROSS PLACE AND TIME

ABHINAV KUMAR

LAUNCHPAD

An imprint of
Srishti Publishers & Distributors

Srishti Publishers & Distributors
A Unit of AJR Publishing LLP
212A, Peacock Lane
Shahpur Jat, New Delhi – 110 049

editorial@srishtipublishers.com

First published by Launchpad,
An imprint of Srishti Publishers & Distributors in 2026

10 9 8 7 6 5 4 3 2 1

For Ritika, the first reader of all my writing.

For Arul, the miracle in our lives.

For my parents and sister, who together instilled in me an enduring love of reading and writing.

Contents

Author's Note

This book is part-culmination of the journey that began on a lazy Sunday afternoon in my hostel in Jodhpur a decade ago. Searching for something to do after a gigantic, stupor-inducing breakfast, I thought of writing a story. It is perhaps too early to say that the rest is history, but that thought, and that story (*Memory*), certainly started it all for me – and that young man would be thrilled to bits to know that one day you would be holding a book of his short stories in your hands.

Since then, writing has been an exhilarating, frustrating, rewarding, overwhelming—but most importantly, permanent—part of life. The efforts are painstaking, the doubts endless; the rewards are fabulously uncertain, and it is lonely work. But I am glad to have persevered, for today I can present this collection with pride and joy, and a quiet belief that there will be more to come.

All That We Carry explores myriad aspects of the human experience through the conduits of different worlds, times, settings, and points of view. In writing these stories, I have explored themes close to my heart, trite situations in which I have discovered the unusual, and subjects that I am knowledgeable about or fascinated by. I hope to have transmitted that fascination, and am convinced that the stories will, at some level—by the underlying theme, a circumstance depicted, or even a casual observation made by a character—resonate with its readers. But above all, and all these lofty goals aside, I hope you simply *enjoy* reading the stories.

By getting yourself a copy of this book, you have tipped your hat to me, to my writing, and have gently told me that you believe in my talents, and that is worth everything. I am sure that, as the threads of my stories gradually unspool over the pages to come, at least a few of them will stay with you for a long time to come.

The Invitation

The invitation looked plain enough. I might have discarded it, but a handwritten scrawl of bright blue at the bottom left of the cream envelope caught my eye. I thrust my usual mail, bills, bank letters, and menus from the local pop-up to one side. On second thought, a wedding invitation was curious enough to merit a closer look. My parents had moved away long ago. The marriages of my near and dear friends, too, had happened in staccato fashion more than a decade back. No relative that I could think of was due.

The blue scrawl was an address, printed in stout, violet-blue letters with serrated edges, seeming to have come from a Parker pen:

W-72, Olive Towers, New Delhi-110072

I blinked. Olive Towers. The forbidden estate. It had seemed to materialise out of rubble within a matter of weeks, just beyond the crumbling northern compound wall of my school. Such naked commercial ambition, jostling for space with a temple of learning, one of my teachers had sniffed, glaring at the contractors—corpulent men who lurked around the school gate with their bright yellow hard hats and *bidis*. Irked by the students' unrelenting interest in the new building and its would-be inhabitants who often drew up in cars that were unimaginably long and sleek, the contractors eventually repaired that poor wall until it was twelve feet high, solid, and topped with barbed wire.

Our curiosity faded soon after, though we sometimes spotted the mysterious residents watching our annual function unfold on the school lawns from balconies that mingled with the skies.

The envelope was unmarked, other than a floral motif and a Sanskrit *shloka* at the bottom right, and a plain white printed label pasted at the centre, bearing my name and address. Mystified, I eased it open with a delicacy reserved for envelopes bearing dividend cheques.

It was one of those long cards, folded thrice over, beginning and ending with prayers and listing the names of two sets of grandparents and several proud uncles of the couple… Were it not addressed directly to me, intrigue of the Olive Towers address notwithstanding, this would be the moment to consign it to the bin. I turned to the middle page, searching for the honorifics announcing the lucky pair.

"Ah… Chiranjeevi Sikander Aiyar," I read aloud. As it happened, an Alexander did feature among my far-flung acquaintances, but not a Sikander.

The parents, perhaps? Maybe an old boss, or colleague, or professor…? As I flipped over the envelope to scan the RSVP, the handwritten address caught my eye again. Definitely a Parker pen. An image flashed in my mind's eye—the iconic purple pen with its silver-topped ink reservoir, the arrow-like clip of the cap. The RSVP revealed more interesting names—Kalis and Ravin—but little else. I decided to move on to other mail, glancing at the address one last time to be certain that it did not trouble my memory.

I'll never use another as long as I live.

The serrated edges… those decidedly squat letters, flowing from the nib of that purple pen, driven by those unusually slender fingers that never quite matched the inelegance of the penmanship… I stood, banging my knee against the edge of the table, and turned the card over.

…the wedding of their granddaughter, Sowbhagyavathy Anushka…

"My Parker pen!" I crowed, then fell back onto my chair, winded.

Anushka Solanki.

Anu.

***

"Not to worry, Sir, we've got you covered for all kinds of special occasions," the young, apron-clad saleswoman at the florist said.

I could have chosen the toothless, grumpy flower-wallah at the local market, but some undefined sense of the gravity of the occasion had brought me here, a snazzy shop teeming with exotic plants and other curiosities.

"A tea or coffee while we look, Sir? Or a juice?"

"Not necessary, thanks."

The house was a mess when I left. Clothes, books and dishes strewn everywhere. I'd hardly had the time or sense to put together a decent outfit, but was gratified to see the saleswoman cast an appreciative eye over my blue cardigan. Never mind that it was borrowed, I've always maintained that it fits me better, hugging my thin frame just right.

"Could you help me with the occasion, Sir?"

"Sorry?"

"What is the special occasion? To help us narrow the choices down?"

"Er..."

I felt for the half-written letter in my pocket, which I'd remembered to stuff into my jeans in the nick of time before heading out. At mid-January, I'd be two months early, but it seemed appropriate.

"Birthday... An old friend."

The saleswoman grinned. "I have just the one you're looking for."

I let her lead, nodding along absently as she gushed about a rather stunning bouquet of white roses, lilies and carnations wrapped in sunny yellow handmade paper. Anu would absolutely hate it.

"Done," I said, cutting the saleswoman off mid-sentence, suddenly feeling like I'd tarried too long. I strode to the payment counter. I didn't, after all, have her phone number, just an address, and was betting on her having stayed in in the mid-afternoon haze.

"Any add-ons, Sir?" The cashier said. "Chocolates, a card? You might also be interested in our extensive collection of luxury stationery…"

"No…" A vintage fountain pen caught my eye. "Is that a Parker?"

The cashier followed my gaze to the display over his shoulder. "That is a superb piece, Sir… although it's a Pierre Cardin. Would you like to have a look?"

"Nah, then let it be."

***

Anu Solanki. Quite the sensation when she joined our school in the summer of Class 9. A curious import from Jodhpur, who had spent her early years of middle school in Hudson, New York (*for the last time, it's in New York STATE, and New York City isn't even the capital*). Just long enough for her to develop a faint American twang and Rs rolled so thickly that they drove the boys in our class crazy.

Much to the girls' annoyance, Anu blended right in. Sprightly and athletic, she took great pleasure in outrunning several boys in our first PE class, instantly winning great admiration and more than a little awe from us.

"A handsome girl," my friend Rajiv had remarked that day. "And you, of all people, get to sit with her!"

A happy alphabetical accident indeed meant that I was to spend the year as her class partner. Scrawny, shy and bookish, it had taken me several days to take a stab at making stammered conversation. Impervious to the fawning and rather predictably male overtures of the larger class, and possibly sensing no threat of the same from the likes of me, she was surprisingly receptive.

Over that summer, we struck up an odd little friendship as class partners sometimes can—a queer intimacy expressed during class hours, but never in the common areas—based on a shared love of classic rock, the Archies, and a fierce attachment to our respective pens. Hers was that purple Parker, promptly replaced if ever lost, and mine, a superbly smooth gel pen called Point-Max, long since out of production.

As hormones descended upon the chicken coop of our grade, an array of hopefuls presented themselves before Anu, each summarily turned away. Before long, I, too, no less susceptible than the best of us, found myself hanging on her every word. While working on a group science project, which was not, unfortunately, allocated in alphabetical order, Rajiv discovered that she lived near the sports club that my family frequented. To my parents' astonishment, I soon began to take long walks in the club grounds, hoping to run into her – a hope unrealised to date.

Blissfully unaware of my feelings, she remarked to me on her birthday the following March that her parents had discovered a gift-wrapped but unmarked Fleetwood Mac cassette in their letterbox. Though Rajiv egged me on to confess, I feigned ignorance along with everyone else.

The ride to Olive Towers was a short one. I grinned as we crossed school, the red-and-white buildings visible over the boundary walls, stolid as ever.

"Address, Sir?" The cab driver asked, slowing down before the imposing gates and pulling over by the security guards' post.

"W-72. Er...Solanki," I added quickly. He repeated the address and name to the guard, who proceeded to speak into the intercom. I began to shift in my seat, frowning at the bouquet which suddenly seemed ostentatious to the point of silliness. Would she be in? Was she actually expecting me? Had I misread the situation? Had she meant to send her address to someone else?

The pause lengthened. The cabbie began to drum his fingers on the steering wheel. Sweat stains began to form under my arms.

The intercom crackled to life, though the voice that spoke was too faint for me to catch. Satisfied, the guard sat back and caused the gates to part. "Straight down, third right."

***

"Amir!"

For a moment, we just stared. You read about such moments in books, fawn over them in movies, but nothing can quite prepare you for the moment you cast your eyes on an old flame whose every movement was once followed out of the corner of one's eye, after a gap of 21 years.

"Anu." She looked elegant, almost regal, wearing the emerald-green sari and necklace of pearls with casual grace. The hair, then cropped short, had grown to waist-length. Once too wiry, reminiscent, by her own admission, of gangly comic-book characters, her frame had filled out, and the folds of the sari hugged her shapely figure.

To fill the silence, I proffered the bouquet, till then clutched by my side, across the foot or so separating us. Thrusting it aside, she threw her arms around my neck.

I stiffened for a moment under her touch, then relaxed, hugging her back with tentative hands.

"When did you grow a moustache?"

"So, I take it you love the bouquet?"

"It's awful," she breathed into my ear, breaking apart without warning. "I can't believe you came."

"Well, you sent the invitation yourself, didn't you?"

"Yes, of course, but I never imagined…"

"What, with that ugly handwriting? Ye of little faith. Congratulations, by the way, before I forget," I said, offering her the bouquet again. "Count this as an early birthday present."

"What, no Fleetwood Mac? Losing our touch, are we?"

"Still a Parker?"

"Always," she said, grinning, and grabbed me by the arm. "Come."

***

And just like that, I was sitting on Anu Solanki's couch, a spot I would have given an arm and a leg to be occupying in the not-too-distant past.

It had seemed impossible even as I had walked in and taken my seat. That this girl, now woman, whose voice I hadn't heard in more than two decades, should be bustling around in this palatial apartment, making me a coffee with her own hands. I watched her maid mill around her, hands twitching, appearing not used to being told to shirk her duties.

My nerves had only grown more frazzled as I approached her door. Impulse had carried me until then, but it wasn't till I laid eyes on her, saw hers widen in recognition, and then dance with pleasure, that I could be sure that I hadn't made a mistake in rushing down.

Even so, and the initial banter notwithstanding, I could only be so sure of myself. A part of me wished I had left it at that, turned around from the door, and returned to the safety of home and the written word. With some terse instructions to the relieved maid, she glided past the island counter in the kitchen and took a seat on the armchair across from me.

"I wasn't sure you'd make the connection."

"I almost didn't, you know. Surely it would have been easier to source my number and get in touch like an ordinary person."

"Why? You never bothered to."

I acknowledged the truth of her statement with a quick bow of the head. The maid walked up and set a tray laden with coffee and cookies down on the table between us, and then, with a quick nod at Anu, disappeared inside.

"What is your number, by the way, now that I'm finally here…"

"It suits you," she said, reaching forward for her cup.

"Sorry?"

"The moustache."

"Thanks." I watched her in suspicion, awaiting the peal of laughter that had been characteristic of nearly all my friends' responses. None came. I took my own cup and took a sip. "It's been a while since I saw that handwriting, but I'd recognise it anywhere."

"I'm glad. It's good to see you."

"I can't say I'm not surprised, though. Didn't imagine I'd figure on your list of invitees."

"Why? Will I not feature on yours?" She leaned forward, staring at me intently.

"I—"

She chuckled, then laughed louder. Taking the hint, I smiled along and said, "Blessed be the day that happens." She shot me an appraising look over the rim of her cup. "Well, who's the lucky guy?" I said, unable to avoid the feeling that I was the one tasked with moving the conversation along.

"Sikander? The son of a family friend." She sat back. "We had been seeing each other on and off for a while and... Eventually, it all just happened."

"It clearly did," I said, waving my arm across the opulent room.

"Yes, it's all a bit much," she stated with a half-smile, as though she had made this observation to herself before.

"It's princely, that's for sure. And fancy you living right next to school!"

"Pretty ironic, isn't it?"

"Ironic? It's perfect!"

"I never did see the big deal about that school. It was at best mediocre."

I opened my mouth in mock horror, though this was something she'd mentioned to me even in Class 10, during one of our last conversations before our separation into the arts and science streams. She missed Hudson, her school there, and felt that it had been more of a home than Delhi could ever be.

"Anyway, the house belongs to his parents. I don't know how long we'll live here."

"Well, what does he do? And, for that matter, how about yourself? Last I heard, you were off conducting research in some biologist's lab at a Mohali institute?"

"Heard from?" She leaned forward once more, resting her elbows on her knees. The curtain of her hair fell over her shoulder, shielding half her face from view. I couldn't help but notice how conventionally attractive she had become. In school, she'd hogged attention because of, not despite, being the charming tomboy, and her occasional moodiness had just added to the intrigue. Here, she looked like a recent entrant into the royal family of some proud Rajput state.

"Hmmm… Not you, that's for sure. Avantika, maybe?"

"I lost touch with her soon after college. Anyway, yes, I was doing that for a while. Now I'm consulting with a couple of pharma companies."

"Sounds tiring."

I had only a couple of sips of my coffee left, and the conversation was beginning to seem rather forced. It suddenly felt foolish to ever imagine that we could devolve into talking about the Archies or our favourite authors or bands anymore. We were too old. And we barely knew each other any longer.

"I'd also heard—"

"How's life at—?"

"You first," she said, as we both paused.

"So, it didn't work out with Kunal, then?"

"You're not seriously gloating?"

"Hard not to gloat after you've heard, *you're great... but I could never like you that way* from the girl of your dreams!"

"Shut up, I did not sound like that!" She said, laughing at my exaggerated American accent, and making as if to throw a cushion at me. The looming insipidity of the meeting seemed to have passed, and I allowed myself to go on, channelling my considered dislike of the only boy she had dated in school. Impossibly tall and muscular, but also rather intelligent and amiable, Kunal was easy for girls to like, and for that very reason, hard for any boy to get along with.

"Anyway, glad that that phase passed. I'm sure Sikander compares very favourably to Kunal."

"Well, if you'd called me the girl of your dreams in your sorry little proposal, maybe I wouldn't have had to date him. Or at the very least, I may have taken longer to say no."

"What? But my proposal channelled all the romantic wisdom of a gawky fifteen-year-old and his cabal of equally wise friends," I said, trying to sound sporting, though I could feel a blush creeping over my cheeks. It was inevitable that this should come up – perhaps this was why she had thought to call me over, albeit in an over-cryptic fashion.

"It's good to see you. I'm glad I never abandoned Parker pens."

"It's great to see you too... You look great," I added at the last moment, avoiding her eye.

She fell silent, and when I looked up again, she was looking out of the floor-to-ceiling windows beside us.

"You were saying then?" I said, picking up my cup.

"Oh? Yes... Just asking how life is at university."

I drained the last sip of my coffee. "Dreadfully dull. I'm up for a sabbatical next session, thinking of taking it up and travelling the world."

"Sounds good." She paused, as if in mid-sentence, then went on, "I, too, yearn to spread my wings and see the world, but have been confined to this dusty city with no prospects on the horizon..."

"Sorry?" The phrase sounded familiar, tickling my memory, but I couldn't place it.

"Never mind. Where are you planning to go?"

That strange lull in the conversation, held off for a few moments by the shared spark of our common past, began to creep in once more. I glanced at her; she seemed quiet and withdrawn, although apparently awaiting an answer.

"I'm not sure. Somewhere by the sea. Kerala, perhaps?"

She folded her arms and nodded but said nothing, simply gazing at me with those luminous brown eyes that seemed to widen whenever she was deep in thought.

"When I am by the sea, I feel infinite... It is an elemental feeling, similar, possibly, to that enjoyed by the first men to lay eyes upon it..."

The room rang with the vibrations of her recitation, the higher-pitched lilt of it. I stared.

"You're not... quoting from..."

"Your letters," said Anu, nodding, but without breaking into the smile I expected.

Flustered, I said, "If only I knew I sounded like a long-suffering failed poet, I would've thought twice about posting them! And the cassettes?" I asked after a moment when she remained silent, curious despite myself.

Without a word, she pointed to a cabinet nearby, towards the foot of which I saw, in neat rows, face-up, the tapes that I had enclosed with some of my earlier letters. Nirvana, The Doors, Scorpions... And sure enough, *Rumours,* by Fleetwood Mac.

"I sent the Abba as a joke, you know," I said.

"It's funny, because I've grown to quite like them," said Anu, brightening up. She began to hum *Super Trouper* while I resisted the urge to get on my knees and leaf through her collection. Even I didn't have several of these tapes of yore—casualties of my parents' overzealous biennial clean-out drives.

"So, you did get my letters… All of them? I'd long begun to assume that the postman used them as kindling."

She nodded, drawing her knees up to her chin in a childlike pose. The sari tented up over her legs and settled around her.

"How did they even reach you? I always sent them to that Siri Fort address!"

"My parents forwarded all my mail, wherever I was. Though I have to say, in recent years, I've had little else, if at all."

I shook my head and grimaced in embarrassment. "Just my silly little tradition, I suppose. Almost an automatic fixture in my life, a reflex. Your birthday's been etched in my brain ever since I left you that anonymous package in March…1995!"

"You didn't write to me last year," Anu spoke quietly, almost inaudibly, from behind her knees.

"Yes, at 35 I thought you—or the postman—may have had enough," I said, chuckling. "And boy, based on those cloying lines you just recited, it sounds like I did everyone a favour."

"Even my parents noticed," she said, sitting up straight, smoothening out the folds of her sari.

"Sorry about that, but you didn't miss much," I said lightly. "Anyway, you've got to tell me more about Sikander! You haven't even told me what he does."

"Oh, this and that. His family has several businesses. Explains the house. They have many others across India, and we're expected to shuttle between them. He himself travels nearly every week, and abroad every other month."

"So here I am, huffing and puffing about a few days in Kerala after decades of service, while you're setting up to join a jet-setting, burgeoning business empire!"

"Yes... He's been asking me to get hitched for a while, you know. But I could never make up my mind."

"That's typical. All my friends—happily married now, by the way—got cold feet."

"I loved receiving your letters. I got them at all odd times of the year, whenever my parents remembered to forward my mail. They've kept me young, in a way."

"Loved them enough never to reply?" She had responded initially, in the couple of years immediately after school. Her letters—notes, to be more accurate—were always short and impersonal.

"I deserve that," said Anu.

I blinked. "I'm sorry... I didn't mean for that to come out quite so sharply."

"No problem," she said, rising in a fluid motion. I stood too. Relief flooded me; the evening sun was slanting in, and I felt it was time for me to put an end to this queer interview and start home. "Let's get some air in the veranda?" Anu stepped to the glass door, leaving the parting congratulations in my mouth.

I joined her and we stepped outside. Forgetting all about ourselves for a moment, I took my time to gaze at the school grounds below. The waning winter sun cast flashes of orange on the yellow-green grass. A few lone figures jogged on the track that flanked the ground. With some embarrassment, I located the corner of the ground where a quizzical, teenage Anu had stood before me one recess, as I stammered out my speech. Casting a sidelong glance at her, I wondered if she remembered the spot. I wished I could point it out and cackle with her, but the reins of the conversation were now firmly in her hands.

"I kept promising myself," she began after a few moments, "to respond around your birthday, after my initial responses tapered off. But your letters were so rich and increasingly descriptive... I never knew where to begin."

I shifted my weight from one foot to another. She went on, "By the time December rolled around, I always felt that it was too late; that March was just around the corner again. So, I ended up just waiting for the next one, letting life intervene in the interim."

"Aw, never mind. Though I daresay I wouldn't have minded knowing sometimes that you were doing all right. But I got bits of information about you from Avantika, or the general school grapevine, every now and then. Anyway," I turned towards her, "trust me, some years, those letters were almost on autopilot, written on the assumption that they would not be read. I wouldn't have been surprised never to hear from you again, if I'm being honest."

"That I can agree with. Written as if they were never to be read... Written almost to oneself. But they weren't, were they?"

I opened my mouth to respond, but fell silent. Suddenly, I couldn't remember at all what I'd written in any of those letters, except the trite annual updates about my life that never took up more than a paragraph or two.

"They were so... intimate, Amir."

My heart began to beat faster, and sure enough, another excerpt followed.

"2011." Five years ago. "I am adrift... I cannot remember the last time I felt peace. Each year brings a new crisis of faith and identity. I do not love my job any longer; the bureaucracy stifles my expression... As for love, although it has been a period of discovery, I find I am not placed much better than earlier—"

"Stop!"

Anu turned to me, an eyebrow raised. Breathing hard, I forced a smile. "Come on, Anu, it's just some philosophical nonsense." My words tumbled out, rushed. "Yes, I agree that it sounds like singing in the shower, dancing when no one's looking. Just some harmless ranting."

"Of course," she said.

"I can't believe you even remember any of them, though I have to admit that if anyone wrote me such high-quality melodrama, even I might remember..."

"I do have a question, though."

I felt my face grow hot, and my babbling tongue subsided. In the ensuing silence, I began to long for the harmless embrace of that intermittent boredom, discontent, even, that we had left inside.

"How come you were never again curious about me?" She asked softly.

"I'm sure I asked—"

"Cursorily. Your letters were otherwise quite self-centred. You lost interest in me."

"And yet, they compare very favourably to all the reams of paper you employed in your responses to me." I drew a sharp breath. Embarrassment and confusion were making me seek shelter in uncharacteristic barbs. I had never expected her to write, whether or not she was reading my letters. Those letters! Birthday wishes followed by overdramatic tosh. I ought not to have subjected Anu—or, for that matter, anyone—to them, but this twisted drama of discussing my peculiar tradition of birthday wishes years and years after the fact... I made an exaggerated show of glancing at my watch.

"Tag Heuer. Not bad for an English professor," Anu remarked.

"A gift."

"Sikander, too, has a fondness. I gifted him a Rado recently. Burnt a hole in my pocket, but he was surprised—and pleased."

Her tone, to my relief and puzzlement, had regained its bantering lilt, reminiscent of her greeting at the door, which felt like part of another life.

"Lucky chap."

"Yes… He really had to ask me several times, you know."

"I'm sure," I responded lightly, unable to bring myself to look at her. "Shall we head back inside? I guess I'd also better call myself a cab…"

***

Back inside, we were different people, chit-chatting like old friends about the upcoming wedding. I learnt that Sikander focused on the export of shawls and other handicrafts, and shared her love of classic rock, but disliked comics. We laughed about his lack of refinement, spending a few moments as I had imagined we would, and perhaps, so had she, when she had scrawled the address on my invitation. In a gracious manner that I quickly came to associate with her in that short exchange, she extracted several promises that I attend each function, and bring anyone I like.

Soon after, my cab was waiting downstairs. The maid reappeared and, having pressed a box of sweets and a fresh, unmarked invitation into my protesting hands, retired back inside. Anu walked me out, complimenting me on my cardigan.

"So, I'll see you next month, at the *mehndi*?"

"Definitely," I said, thinking I'd disentangle my thoughts on my RSVP over the next few weeks.

I summoned the lift. "Can't wait to meet Sikander," I said, watching the number rise on the lift panel and willing it to 7.

"Two questions, actually," Anu said, stepping into my eyeline. "Are you still adrift in love, or better placed now?" Her tone was mocking, but her breathing quick and shallow, and eyes eager.

I took an involuntary step back. "Anu, I am sor—"

"No, don't," she said, turning away.

The lift arrived. I stepped in with gratitude and faced her, ready with my goodbyes.

"Just the one thing, Amir," said Anu, holding the door. I paused in pressing the button for the ground floor. My phone began to ring in my pocket. "The letters. They need to stop."

"I—y-yes…"

"I'll be a married woman next month," she stated, again with the air of it being an observation she had made to herself before.

"Yes."

"No need to write one for this year… That is, if you haven't already posted it," she said, with a sudden, bitter laugh.

My hand dropped to my pocket, but I made as if to pick up my phone.

"See you next month?" She repeated, letting go of the doors, which began to shut.

"Of course. Bye, Anu!"

The doors shut as she raised a hand to wave goodbye.

***

On my way to the gate, I paused near a bench and whipped out the half-written letter. With a racing heart, I began to read:

Dear Anu,

Happy birthday!

I do wonder if my letters reach you, etc.

It has been a dull year, and I can't wait to go on vacation, etc.

And then, sure enough:

I am writing to tell you that I have finally met someone, after several tumultuous years and disappointments, and you will laugh when you find out that…

Shaking my head, I tore up the sheet and tossed it in the bin nearby before jogging to the gate to head home.

***

The shower was running when I got back. Placing my key in its holder, I sidestepped the suitcase and, ignoring the mess in the kitchen, made straight for the half-finished wine bottle from last night. Pulling out two glasses, I brought them to the table.

"Good trip?" I called out, pouring myself a glass, only half-hopeful of being heard over the shower. I waited a moment, then shrugged and took a big sip.

Anu fucking Solanki. I shook my head.

"Sorry for all the chaos, I'll pick it up…" Arun said, dripping wet, dressed in just a towel. "Hey, I've been looking for that cardigan everywhere!"

I grinned. He leaned down to plant a kiss on my head. "Isn't it too early for wine?"

"Not today, no."

"Tough day, huh?" He straightened up and began towelling his hair.

"You'd never believe it if I told you. But maybe you'd better sit down for this one," I said, dragging a chair and reaching for the bottle.

Gaze

She rose with the sun as always. They'd never really talked about who between them would be the early riser, but Meghna had taken it on without demur. *Aman, of course, had no reason to complain,* she thought with a smile, feasting her eyes on his naked, brown body sprawled over the white of the covers.

Maaji, herself an early riser, had been pleased, though she had never said so. When Meghna had just entered the house, an unspoken competition raged between them. She would often find Maaji waiting in the kitchen, contemplating the marble-topped counter as it lit up with the first rays of the day. Eventually, as Meghna turned up earlier and earlier, day after day, the older woman had to concede. It was a small victory, but significant nonetheless.

A working wife?

She will neglect your kitchen and your home; just wait and watch.

Don't you make enough money for the both of you?

Meghna put the water to boil and reached for the tea leaves. Without sugar but with ginger for Maaji, without ginger but with sugar and *elaichi* for Aman. With well-practised hands, she worked the two stoves separately, bringing the two cups of tea to a boil together. Movement sounded from the inner room soon after.

"Slept well, *beta*?" Maaji asked, ever courteous, taking her seat at the dining table. They liked each other as much as two people could without becoming friends.

"Yes, Maaji," Meghna said, taking care to set the cup down without spilling a drop. "Hope you did too."

Her mother-in-law offered no reply, and murmuring a prayer, she raised the cup to her lips. A slurpy sip, then silence. A sigh. And finally, a slight curve of the lips. Maaji reached for the cup once more.

"Enjoy your *chai*, Maaji," Meghna said, turning away to hide a smile as she replayed various versions of this little ritual in her mind's eye.

***

She'd played it safe for many days, she mused, stepping into her wardrobe. And she'd been working out. It was the day for a dress. She reached for a gorgeous black specimen. Knee-length, of course. But sexy nonetheless.

Is there no dress code at her office?

She slipped into the dress after her bath and surveyed herself in the full-length mirror. A bit more work on the hips, perhaps, she thought, running a critical eye over herself. But it worked otherwise. The diamond earrings—the smaller, understated ones—to go with this. Yes, definitely.

"You're dressed for a special day," Aman said, stepping out of the bathroom.

"Aman, you're dripping water all over the floor again."

"Sorry, sorry." Without a hint of shame, he continued to walk across the room.

"But yes, I felt like a dress today," Meghna said, turning to face him.

"Good, you look fabulous."

"You say that every day."

He flashed her a lascivious grin. "But you know I like dresses in particular."

"You have no shame, Aman Singh," Meghna said, reaching for her bag.

"I'll take that as a compliment. So, I assume that it'll be a special night as well?"

She stuck her tongue out at him as she left the room.

***

The cab was late. She watched the traffic pass by, inhaling the noxious fumes of the city as it moved. Aman had offered to drop her off, of course, but her office was on the other side of town. Little beads of perspiration began to form in her armpits. She responded like she always did—by setting down her arms as close to her sides as she could.

The cab arrived just as she was about to cancel the booking. The driver was both apologetic and pleasant. She asked him to crank up the AC and sat back, relaxing as the cool air restored her poise. The driver pulled into the traffic, taking his time to adjust the mirror.

Aman, can you call me?

Everything okay?

Yes, I just need you to call me. This guy is acting a little weird.

That was years ago. Today, she simply waited to catch his eye and flashed her pearly whites at him. He stopped fiddling and focused on the road.

Her phone began to buzz as she neared the office. A new project, a flood of emails. Good. She'd been expecting to get staffed on something big for a while now. Her heart beat faster as she digested the lowdown. This could be career-defining.

"Thank you, madam," the cabbie said as she stepped out. *Nice try,* she thought, slamming the door shut.

***

"You've seen the emails, I hope?" Rishi looked more anxious than usual.

"Of course," Meghna said, setting her laptop down.

"I didn't expect this matter to drop into our laps, to be honest," he continued, wringing his hands.

"I've taken a spin through the documents. It'll be some long hours, but I'm on top of it."

Rishi broke into a relieved smile. Meghna liked him and forgave him for the times his jumpy ways got on her nerves.

"Expecting the client any moment now," he said, eyes darting between the door and his watch. "And our man is late as usual." He paused. Meghna noticed his eyebrow twitching uncontrollably—the tic that inevitably surfaced when stress got the better of him. "I know you haven't had much time," he said, flashing her his best, beseeching Bambi look. For once, it seemed to be playing into her hands. "But will you—?"

"Sorry I'm late," Prithvi said, breezing in. "And may I introduce," he continued, with an exaggerated wave of the hand, "the lovely Mr Kothari. I happened to run into him in the lift. We've had a brief chat and I've assured him of the best of our services."

***

"Thank you very much, Prithvi and Meghna," Mr Kothari said, a few hours later. "I do apologise for the short notice, but I'm glad to see that Rishi has engaged his best resources for us."

"As promised, Sir," Rishi said.

"We expect the first motion to come up for hearing by 11 am tomorrow," Meghna said, scanning through the files.

"Excellent, the quicker the better," Mr Kothari said, rising. "Just one last thing, then, who will be arguing for us?" He glanced at Prithvi, then Meghna, letting his eyes slide down to her bosom.

Meghna's eyes bored into Rishi's skull.

"Prithvi will be first chair."

"Excellent, excellent," Mr Kothari said. Meghna nodded at him and smiled, as if it was all pre-arranged. "I'll see you in court tomorrow morning then."

We talked about this, Rishi. We had an agreement.

I know, I know, look, it was a tough call to take for me as well.

Yes, I can see that you're the real victim here.

Look, they sent a conservative guy; they have these notions. You know how it is.

"So, I'll see you at 10, Prithvi. Courtroom 1." Meghna swept out of the room before either man could open his mouth.

***

She liked her desk for how secluded it was, cornered off from the rest of the bullpen by a translucent glass column. The solitude sheltered her.

She sat very still. *You know how it is.* Out of the corner of her eye, she watched Rishi clap Prithvi on the back as they left the conference room, eyes bright with manly laughter. Staring at nothing in particular on her screen, she imagined gouging Mr Kothari's eyes out before they had a chance to travel, uninvited, over her body.

Her hands clenched into fists of their own volition. Fixating on them, she imagined landing a pleasing blow to Rishi's jugular, robbing him of his voice before he had a chance to say the words. He would fall, spluttering, gasping for a wisp of air, as Prithvi fled and Mr Kothari screamed, waving his arms in search of light, bleeding scarlet rivulets onto the Persian carpet—

"Smoke?" Sneha looked uncertain. Meghna blinked to rid her eyes of the glaze and rearranged her features.

"Sure."

I didn't know you smoked! You always seemed so—

There was never an end to that sentence. She half-listened to Sneha yap about her day, nodding intermittently.

"Oh, by the way, I saw the three of you huddled up in there with Kothari. Huge client! How did it go?" Her junior colleague looked at her with earnest, admiring eyes. Sneha's naiveté, her unshakeable faith in the goodness of the world, always made Meghna smile.

"Oh, you know how it is," she replied a few moments later, much to Sneha's bewilderment. "Shall we get back to work?"

***

No driver was willing to go that far. She decided to take the metro halfway. A deep dive into work had distracted her for the rest of the day, but now, as she approached the security screening, she slipped back into her reverie and out of her body. It was involuntary now. She hadn't spoken to anyone about this, not even to Aman. She could never find the words to describe it.

She could no longer feel them.

The young, smartly dressed woman steps behind the security curtain. She stares past the leering guard who frisks her, and does not flinch when she gives her thigh an extra pat to punish her for her bare legs. She catches the last train out, mingling with the midnight crowd of borderline drunks and adventurous teenagers.

*Snickers. Rapacious glances. A gleeful whistle. A sharp, mechanical *click*. Muffled laughter as the offending cell phone is passed around. She makes her way to the women's coach. A couple of young girls catch her eye and smile weakly, in solidarity. She cannot conjure up any sympathy. She moves on and sits in an empty row.*

The train came to a screeching halt. Meghna jerked and focused on the green letters above the doors, which announced her stop. The coach was deserted. She willed herself to rise and stepped out onto the platform. A few sniggering teenagers had disembarked from the adjacent coach. One of them bowed to her in an elaborate greeting as she passed. Eyeing them with distaste, she quickened her steps and hurried to the exit.

***

Her last mile cab driver was an old man. He, too, fiddled with the rear-view. She could not tell whether it was genuine. Shutting her eyes, she dug her nails deep into her thighs, willing him to get her home fast. The tiny pricks of pain told her that her flesh yet clung to her. Her body felt hot, heavy.

"Reached, madam," the driver said, not long after. When she made no move, he caught her eye in the mirror and smiled. She smiled back thoughtlessly, mumbled her thanks, and tumbled out.

"How was your day?" Aman said, planting a kiss on top of her head.

"Usual," she replied. He took her hand and led her to the bedroom. She relaxed with each step, allowing the warmth of his presence to draw her in its embrace.

"Didn't realise it was going to get so late," he said, stroking the small of her back.

"Busy day, I guess."

"All the more reason for a special ending." Aman winked. "Let's get you out of this dress, it's all crumpled anyway."

"Let me get into something more comfortable," Meghna said, getting to her feet. Aman fell back on the bed and propped himself up on his elbows, anticipation bringing colour rushing into his cheeks. She locked eyes with him, willing her arms to move.

Maaji's querulous stare.

The morning cabdriver's stolen glances.

Rishi's beseeching eyes. Kothari's careless glimpse and summary dismissal. Prithvi's triumphant gaze.

The insolence of the bowing youth.

Aman's hungry, expectant eyes.

"Aman, can you do me a favour?"

He looked up, bemused.

"Can you look away while I change?"

Samaritan

He caught my eye the moment I alighted. Perhaps it was just good business sense; after all, my colourful, well-fitting clothes must have given me away as a metro dweller. My co-passengers were anything but. Heavy, multi-coloured turbans, luxuriant moustaches, rainbow saris.

As the conductor began to haul out luggage from the womb of the bus, I could see the man loitering nearby, seeming to zero in on me and the few foreign tourists who had chosen to travel by bus. I took him to be an auto-wallah who fancied himself the carrier of the discerning tourist, for he kept his peace while other peddlers swarmed around, calling out their wares.

One by one, my fellow travellers identified their luggage and set off into the city, some in sputtering rickshaws and some on foot. I was convinced, as usual, with every passing moment, that my luggage, over all else, had been flicked.

This, despite the dentured conductor having extracted a dubious 'luggage fees' of ten rupees, and having scribbled something onto my suitcase in white chalk before shoving it in with the rest. Perhaps that was just to mark me out as a gullible fool whose luggage deserved to be looted more than those who had resisted this made-up levy.

A foreign couple stood nearby, pink faces shining with perspiration, a mound of leather suitcases in tow. Looking at me once more, the man I had taken to be an auto-wallah gave me a wry smile and a little shrug. His meaning couldn't have been more obvious—white skin first. He made a beeline for them, whipping out his own turban and adjusting it so that it sat on his greasy curls just right.

He accosted them with a traditional greeting, which was met with glances of just suspicion. But he then played his trump card—switching to delightfully fluent English, which had the desired effect. The couple broke into bemused smiles and listened with some interest.

"I am sure you have made arrangements, Sir and Madam. But I assure you, the experience my trusty vehicle and I have to offer cannot be found in an air-conditioned taxi." Bemused turned to amused.

"Not convinced? No problem. I am just asking you to give me a chance. If you don't like it, I can bring you back right here. And you can carry on with your taxi for the rest of your trip."

"How much—?" The lady began, but the gentleman made a clucking sound, and she fell silent.

"Oh, come on, Sir," the man said, tugging at his ear, where a copper-coloured stud glinted in the pale moonlight.

"That's quite all right, my man, our car will be here any moment."

The lady pursed her lips and looked away, but that appeared to be that. Undaunted, the man, a redoubtable Marwari it seemed, said, "Perhaps you will reconsider if your car doesn't arrive in five minutes."

The gentleman said nothing and looked around, evidently hoping to bore the gallant local into submission.

"*Arre yaar*," the conductor snapped, emerging from the luggage chute. "Whose suitcase here?!"

The couple and the Marwari turned to me; the Marwari winked. I started, face reddening, and reached out. The chalk had rubbed off and scattered, but the suitcase was unmistakably mine.

"*Shukriya*," I said to the grumpy conductor and turned around before he could demand another tenner. Friends had recommended a suitable lodge for solo travellers; my parents had offered to book me into a good hotel (*we'll make it the rustic kind if you're so fussed*), but I'd put up a staunch resistance. Besides, none of the good hotels were close to the areas worth exploring. I'd managed to book myself into the lodge in the end.

As I mapped the lodge on my phone, I surveyed the scene, free from worry about luggage theft. The Marwari had opened his mouth to renew his pitch when a panting, uniformed man ran up, his bright cap askew, holding up a board for a Mr and Mrs Napier.

The gentleman snapped at him for being late, cutting through his profuse apologies as he bent double and tried to gather all their luggage in one go. The lady looked relieved but shot the Marwari a wistful look. He took the lost opportunity with surprising grace, smiling and shrugging at her.

My phone buzzed—the lodge was less than 500m away. On impulse, I decided to walk it, resisting the sudden urge to bid the couple goodbye as they followed the heaving chauffeur towards a gleaming Audi. I wondered if the evidently well-to-do couple had taken the bus only to have an authentic traveller's experience. Then again, perhaps, like me, they were partial to the road, finding it cumbersome to bother with flights for relatively short distances.

"What a shame," said a voice beside me as I strode in the Google-dictated direction. The Marwari had fallen into step with me.

"What?" I said, stepping aside, not a little wary. Though not far from my destination, it was night, and the road was quite deserted.

"I thought I had them." He sighed. "Well," he continued, with the air of one who was resigned to settling for second best. "And *your* destination is—?"

"Don't need a ride, but thank you," I said, stepping ahead.

"But you seem to need *that* to tell you where to go." He pointed a disdainful finger at my phone. "They get it wrong sometimes, you know. Tourists, even Indians, will always need *asli* locals." He stuck out his chin and kept up with me.

I appreciated his tenacity, but I was beginning to get irritated. Surely, he could wait around for the late-night buses to offer his services, whatever they were. Perhaps he had taken encouragement from my listening in to his conversation with the Napiers. *That'll teach you to eavesdrop,* I thought to myself severely.

"*Waise,* where are you from? First time in Rajasthan?"

"Agra," I lied.

"As if," he said, laughing. "Dolce & Gabbana sunglasses in Agra? Definitely Delhi-Bombay."

My face turned hot again, and I glared at the offending sunglass case strapped to my backpack.

"What are you doing here? Didn't get a good hotel like the *firang* couple?" I noticed that he'd dropped the Queen's English and was speaking with the 'Indian' twang invented by foreigners making TV shows for other foreigners. I wondered if that's how he'd picked up the language.

We turned into a narrower lane, devoid of activity. An owl hooted. A dog turned a corner and stared at us with keen yellow eyes. I wondered if he was right and my phone had it wrong. Perhaps I should have taken up my parents' offer for the first night and gone hunting for the lodge in bright sunshine. Or I could have just taken a rickshaw, piped up a small, accusing voice in my head.

"I'm really all right, thank you," I said, though suddenly grateful for his presence. He was busy stuffing a large paan into his mouth and took no notice. I walked on. 300m to go.

"Sorry, the fool gave me the wrong one today," he said thickly, catching up a few moments later.

"My lodge is right down the next road, you can carry on now," I said.

"*Nahin,* I insist. You're in our city for the first time," he said, the presumption entirely accurate, though I had made no response to his earlier question. "Alone also—this *solo* travel is becoming a fashion among you all, eh?" He did not wait for me to reply. "The least the best guide in the city can do is to drop you at your hotel."

Saying nothing, I walked on, hiding a smile. Though unsolicited, it made for a good beginning to a promising trip. A few friends had wanted to come along, but I'd insisted on going solo—perhaps to seek out just these kinds of experiences—a night trek through the winding lanes of Udaipur's old city with a jolly Marwari in tow?

I shot a sidelong glance at my companion. He seemed harmless enough, though I slipped a hand in my pocket and patted the pepper spray my mother had pressed into my hands at the door.

"You've come at a good time," he was saying with genuine enthusiasm. "So have those *goras*." He sighed. "I really thought I had them there, but that donkey turned up at just the wrong time." I grinned, instantly regretting it when he laughed out loud. "I know, I was just seconds away from snapping them up, they leave fat tips, you know."

"You've been a guide all your life?"

"Twenty years," he said, drawing himself up to his full height. "First in Jodhpur, where I'm from, then I got bored there and got myself here. I know every corner of this city. You must visit the popular spots, of course," he went on, as we turned another corner. 150m to go.

City Palace, Lake Pichola, Jag Mandir, Fatehsagar. But you must retain me for a private tour of the old city. I'll show you all of its secrets, places *that* thing," he jabbed at my phone, "will never tell you about."

"Ok, sure," I said, hoping that the insincerity of my voice would disabuse him of any notion that such a thing would come to pass. A short walk was all very well, but I had no intention of doing a guided tour anywhere.

"*Arre,* where did you say your hotel was?" He frowned for the first time.

"Right down here," I said. Had I been foolish not to ward him off earlier?

He gave me a strange look, up and down, as if seeing me for the first time once more. I swallowed, but held his gaze as coolly as I could, watching out for any sudden movements.

"We must turn back," he said after a moment, his voice low.

My heart began to pound against my chest. I kicked myself for going along with his antics. I should have hailed a rickshaw when I had the chance.

"We must turn back!" He cried, stopping under a flickering street light.

"Why?" I said, slowing down. Just about 100m to go. It'll be fine, it'll be fine, I repeated to myself in my head.

"You cannot stay here! I'm the best guide in the city, and I'm telling you, it's not safe."

The lodge had excellent ratings, and my friends had recommended it highly. Very hip. Just the kind of place I was looking for. And yet… The man seemed earnest enough. He gazed at me, tugging at his ear again.

"I'm staying at a good lodge," I countered. "I'm sure it'll be fine." I looked around furtively to make sure this was not some kind of elaborate trap.

"I insist that we turn around. I'll find you a good place in the heart of Udaipur. You should have told me you were staying in this area," he said, throwing me an accusing look, also looking around with mistrust in his eyes.

The dint of fear in his eyes intrigued me. "What is wrong with this area?"

He stepped a bit closer, and I instinctively reached for the pepper spray.

"This," he said, a tinge of impatience in his voice. "This is where..." He hesitated. I wondered if I would hear a chilling story of some local spirit that roamed the lanes on moonlit nights. "You don't belong here," he went on. "This is where *they* live," he finished, his voice just above a whisper.

"Who?"

He shook his head and thrust his chin down the lane. I followed his gaze to a crumbling minaret.

It's right next to a small mosque. You'll see a red door with 'Udai Guest House' plastered over it. That's the one. Careful not to miss it.

I grinned as relief flooded through me.

"You must reconsider," my companion pleaded as I resumed walking with confident steps.

"*Arre bhaiyya ji,*" I said, newfound enthusiasm in my voice and a spring in my step. "It's a good area only."

He shook his head again, but followed. I heard him mumble about foolish city kids with new-fangled ideas about things they didn't understand.

"You won't feel safe here," he declared, falling into step with me again. "I know you all, you come looking for some kind of, how do you say it? *Authentic* experience. And within a day, you lose your nerve and run back to your city."

I let him whine it out. I imagined he had commission arrangements with multiple hotels, so I could understand part of his frustration. The other part, it seemed, actually stemmed from concern for his understanding of a lonely metro kid in an unknown city. It was touchingly gallant and amusing. I grinned again as we passed the minaret.

"I could show you multiple guest houses that are equally *authentic,*" he grumbled, drawing a bit closer to me. I stayed my course; it was clear that I had the upper hand, a fact confirmed by his having switched entirely to Hindi and the manner in which his head twitched from side to side, as if expecting an all-out attack at any moment.

"Never mind, I'm sure this will be good enough for me," I said as I spotted the red door. The old city had swallowed us up; the bus depot seemed miles away. I couldn't hear any sounds of the road.

"That's the one?" My companion asked, adjusting his turban. I nodded.

"Well, never mind," he said with another sigh. "I tried to warn you. I'd promised you I'd drop you off at your hotel, and I have, even if it's here. At least you won't tell your friends Rajasthani guides don't keep their promises."

"Never," I said with a smile as we stepped up to the door. I caught faint strains of ambient music from within.

"Well, madam *ji*, at least you had the services of the best guide in Udaipur for free," the Marwari said with a nervous laugh, adjusting his turban. "I do hope you'll ask for me tomorrow. Here is my card," he said, whipping it out and thrusting it at me before I could refuse. "And be careful," he hissed, looking over his shoulder.

"Adhirath Singh…" I struggled to read the Devanagari script in the poor light.

"Bagri. Adhirath Singh Bagri, Udaipur's No. 1 Guide," he said, albeit with less bravado than earlier. He extended his hand. "*Aur aapka?*"

I flashed him a broad grin and gave him a firm shake.

"Very nice to meet you, Bagri *ji*, and thank you for keeping me company. My name is Sadiya Khan."

Veil

He could recall the exact moment. The merchant's fat lips, pulled over pearly teeth, mouthing a warning that slid past his ears. He had eyes only for the oilskin money bag steadily extending in his direction. Not again, he had promised himself in that single moment's hesitation that had stayed his hand. Never again.

It had taken four meetings with the merchant and four liberal cups of precious wine to convince him. He had had to sidestep and downplay the stories, the rumours, which, like creeping vines, followed him from one town to the next. The doubt lasted but a fleeting moment. An electric current ran through him as he felt the weight of the bag, shook it ever so slightly to savour the clink of the coins within. He felt infinite; the possibilities were limitless, and the chance of default was negligible.

A clang on the bars.

"Up with yer, bastard."

Sitting still, he stared at the leering guard. Silence, he had come to learn, was infuriating to these despicable men. Several of them had been itinerant mercenaries once, swords for hire, and were now serving the Crown quite by chance. This often brought a smug tinge of righteousness to their bearing, which was unmistakable in the guard's manner.

The clanging continued. James said nothing, but twiddled his thumbs and stared at the single shaft of light that streamed through a tiny, misshapen window above, the only promise of the continued existence of the outside world.

"Can't hide behind silence no more," the guard said, pausing his orchestra and standing back, a sardonic smile on his face. It broadened when James looked up, curiosity breaking his composure.

"Got company from tonight, haven't ye." James's mouth grew dry. The only solace he'd had in all his time in prison had been his solitude; the freedom to plot and plan undisturbed, to give flight to the numerous ventures that constantly unfolded in his mind. He wanted no companion; his pride, intact even in incarceration, would not permit him to place himself among the hordes of murderers, thieves and brigands that peopled His Majesty's prisons.

"'E'll set you right, 'e will. Frightening bugger, from what I hear," the guard sneered. James felt a shadow cross his face. Bluff or not, the guard was taking his cruel pleasure in James' evident discomfort.

Sighing, he fingered the gap between a couple of loose bricks on the floor. A coin glinted in the dark chasm. He pushed himself along the floor, feigning interest in the guard's words, so that he crossed the bricks and, with his right arm behind him, noiselessly parted them, extracted the coin and closed the gap. With his left hand, James beckoned to the guard.

"What's this then?" The guard said, eyes darting about in suspicion.

"Sir," James began in a voice of greasy supplication, drawing close to the bars. "I am a man of business, of commerce, a trader, if you will."

"An' a damned sight bad one," the guard spat out. "Lost all yer money, didn't ye? Yers and everyone else's, and it's landed you here under my nose!"

"Er, yes. Nevertheless, I am still one accustomed to a certain kind of company, or none at all."

The guard said nothing. James followed his greedy eyes to the coin clutched in his right hand, as he gesticulated mildly with his left.

"I would, then," James went on, knowing well that his words were now lost, "be grateful to continue my time here alone. And I was hoping a discerning man such as yourself," the guard looked up sharply, "could help me in this matter," James finished, careful to maintain evenness of tone.

The cell rang with the silence that followed the longest conversation it had witnessed in weeks. The guard appeared to be weighing the offer, which James hoped was a good sign.

"Yer a tricky feller," the guard said after a few moments. "Stealin' and thievin'." James looked up. "But I suppose I could do yer this favour. It'll take me some work, it will, and God help me swallow why any devil care to be alone in this dungeon. But I can try."

James set his lips into a tight smile. "Hand over, then," the guard said. James wondered for a moment if he had been hasty—if, rather than betting on the dubious scruples of this oaf, he should have just prayed for a companion not unlike himself.

"Give it to me!" The guard roared. James sighed and slipped his hand through the bars. The guard pounced. A moment later, James was the poorest he had ever been.

***

He slept badly that night and woke to a throbbing head. The depth of his sleep early on in his incarceration had surprised him, almost as if his soul were aware of the possibility of it. The dirt, the taunts of the guard, the stench of the privy—a hole in the corner that was cleaned twice a week—none affected him as much as he had always dreaded.

He rubbed his eyes, inhaled the miasma of the room, sighed and rose to urinate. The guard's slow, heavy footsteps sounded behind him.

"So yer up then." James ignored him, feeling that their relationship ought to revert to its original state after last night's hiccup. "Had me a nice ale last night. I suppose I'll have to thank yer." The guard's chair creaked as he lowered himself onto it. "But I won't. Got more work on me hands from today, haven't I?"

Waves of hearty laughter rushed through the prison bars and crashed into James's back.

"Business! Commerce!" The guard roared, relishing his mirth. James thrust his trousers into place and shuffled back to his chosen corner. "He'll be here soon, and he'll set yer right. About time yer had some company, though nobody would have that thug over for tea, y'know?" The guard leaned back and slapped his thigh.

James turned away and, clenching his fists, shut his eyes. The sounds of the guard's person, words, and laughter faded away. With coin lost and solitude slipping away, everything precious had finally deserted him. For the first time, he wondered if these damp walls were to form his home till the end of his days. He slumped onto the wall closest to him and slept.

***

He woke to a pair of eyes gazing into his from across the cell. Bright, fidgety, brown eyes. They flitted from his eyes to his face to his body and the rest of the cell, finally coming back to rest on him. Head cocked to the side, wisps of grey hair smoothed over carelessly, the man was shrivelled and old, his bones jutting out of elbows that hugged his knees to his chest.

James stole a quick look outside. The guard's chair was empty. The fading light from the window told him that dusk had fallen. He leaned back and trained his eyes on the man, who had turned away, revealing a glimpse of what had once been a fine cloak on his back.

"My name is Mr Montagu, and that is what you may call me." Crisp words, spoken with a diction that belied his bedraggled bearing. James shot him a closer look. "Having said that, you will excuse me for being impolite. I do not care for you and never shall. I see you have chosen your corner, and this shall be mine. Do not cross over, and I never shall."

James gaped, then stifled a smile and glanced to the heavens in thanks. Standing abruptly, he walked a few brisk steps, exulting in his youth and his evident strength relative to that of the shell of the man before him, who, as if to underscore James's newfound sense of power, shrank deeper into himself. He would waste away within days.

"Having said that—" Montagu began again, only his eyes visible above his knees. James glanced at the pathetic figure. "Don't you know I'm the king of England?"

James threw back his head and laughed. A whimper sounded from Montagu's corner, and James only laughed harder.

***

In the days that followed, James could have paid the guard back for his taunts over the previous six months, but advised himself against it. The guard, to his credit, had sensed James's renewed spirits and began to keep to himself, even desisting from giving Montagu the same welcome he had reserved for James. At some level, James felt that they were united in sympathy for the poor man.

After their initial exchange—if he could think of it as one—Montagu said not a word for a week. He barely ate or drank, and, but for the unavoidable reminders of the other's presence in the cell—ragged breathing, an active bladder and runny bowels—James may well have been alone.

Yet, his initial relief at a harmless companion had faded. He struggled to return to the plotting and planning that had filled his early days in the cell. Though he was loath to admit it, he feared that his convictions in himself, in his ambitions, his destiny, were receding with the passing days. He began to sleep more than he could ever remember, hoping to pass his days in a stupor that avoided all thought.

It'll be a year, the young lawyer, green behind the ears—the best the last of his coin had afforded him—had called out as he was led away. *Keep patient for a year, and you'll be where you belong.*

James's eyes flickered open to the unsettling black of the cell and the guard's soft snores. An odd choice of parting words. *Where he belonged.* He'd lived in more places than he could remember; prospered and thrived in some, fled from others. He had no home, had run away from the few that had tried to box him in, and was yet proud of it.

A careless quip, surely, coming from a person of no consequence in his life. But the more it settled in his thoughts, the more it pricked him. Surely, the accursed youth had not believed that James' lot was with thieves and delinquents. *Borrowing is not a sin. Failed ventures are but a virtue.* His own words, oft-mumbled in the solitude of the cell, felt feeble, weak. He shut his eyes.

He had no attachment to this town, despised its simple folk—shepherds and woodcutters, he'd called them, to hearty laughter at a gathering long ago—and cursed himself for the hundredth time for returning. If only he had not come back. Had he kept running…had he not asked to meet the same merchant… *But it was only to ask for more time.* If only he had sensed it. *The room was too empty, the merchant too jovial.* Had he refused the wine…had he paused after a sip…had he preserved some strength to fight. *Right where you belong.*

He jolted awake, hitting his head against the cold stone.

"It's better to sleep lying down, you know."

James blinked. He could see nothing, but was certain he'd heard his first words in over a week.

"I couldn't see anything. But I heard a thud and a gasp. We have nothing in here," Montagu paused, rather dramatically, James felt. "So, I assumed you hit your head."

Pondering these words, James rubbed his head and hoped the wound would heal in a few days.

"It happens, you know, when you slump, sitting against that dirty wall like you often do."

"Well, I'm sorry Your Highness doesn't approve of my sleeping habits," James snarled.

Montagu laughed. "Just some advice. Discard it if you wish."

It hadn't taken too many words for James to feel like he was speaking to a completely different person. Even on the first day, the diction had been remarkable, and the man had some trappings of wealth. But James had assumed that he was a degenerate, a lunatic who had been carted off to prison by some scheming relatives. Or some equally torrid tale. For the first time since entering Montagu's companionship, James' curiosity was piqued.

"Who are you?" Montagu asked simply, before James could speak again.

"I would ask the same of you, Sir."

"Did I not introduce myself? My apologies, I haven't, er, been myself of late." He spoke with an almost regal bearing, James thought, wondering how this strange creature had ended up in this town of simpletons, let alone in this cell.

"My name is Edward Montagu. And you are, er?"

"James." His eyes were getting heavy, though James told himself that fighting sleep for a few more minutes might prove rewarding.

"Er, well, right then, James. Good to know you, though I wish it were under more pleasant circumstances."

James snorted his agreement, feeling unusually reticent. He felt that Montagu would, very soon, divulge a great deal more on his own than if he led with questions.

Montagu sighed. "I suppose not even in a gaol cell will I find someone who cares to speak to a madman."

"You're aware, then?"

"Not always. But I suppose I was in a state when I was brought here."

"Yes."

"I do apologise if I frightened you."

"On the contrary, I feel it is I who might say that to you."

"Well, of course you are forgiven." Montagu seemed to beam, reveling in the fact of their conversation. James felt a little less interested than before. If he were just a lonely madman—

"Who are you?" James echoed the question that he had deflected.

"An unfortunate man."

James chuckled. A deflection, yet not an untruth. "Show me a man who does not say these words in prison—"

"And I will show you... God?" Montagu returned his laughter, then lapsed into silence.

James felt his smile fade. His head throbbed a little less than before, and his eyes, soothed for once by the dark, silent room, began to close.

"Just one more chance." The hoarse whisper registered on James some moments after the words were spoken. He blinked. "One more chance. A fair hearing by the family. A little more time." No louder than a whisper, but the words were clear and urgent.

Raving, James thought. He lay down, shutting his eyes.

"One-more-chance-some-more-time-a-hundred-coin-more. And just, just a little forbearance from the creditors."

James jerked awake and sat up.

"Montagu?"

The only sound from within the cell was Montagu's ragged breathing.

"Sir? The coin? The creditors?"

The breathing deepened, became harsher. James heard the older man shuffle around in his corner.

"Sir?" James whispered. "What did you just—?"

"My name is Mr Montagu, and that is what you may call me." Clear, crisp, hollow words.

Disgusted, James lay back as silence descended on the cell once more.

***

Montagu slept as if in a trance for the next two days. Just enough time for James to convince himself that he had begun to hallucinate; that night, that conversation, being the first instance. The introduction of a companion had harmed him after all, though more insidiously than he had first imagined.

Physical pain may be easier to bear, James thought, stroking the now-dry bump on his scalp. So, not everything was imagined.

An evening storm lashed the walls of the prison with sheets of rain. Water dripped into the cell from a crack in the ceiling, forming a puddle in the centre. James shivered, alone in the cold draft. The guard, increasingly subdued, had taken to spending hours on end away from duty.

No doubt ensconced in a blanket by a roaring fire, James thought, hugging himself in bitter silence.

"A bit wet, isn't it?" James froze. "Have I startled you?" That same clipped accent. Words loud enough to be heard above the wind, intended to be understood and responded to.

"Mr Montagu?" James said, turning to the older man who was sitting up.

"James."

If he was slipping into hallucination once more, James thought, *then his mind was in fine form.* The man simply couldn't have known his name if not for the earlier conversation. Why, even the guard didn't refer to him by name, just spat out his chosen abuse.

"How do you feel now?"

"Me? It's *you* who's been sleeping like the devil—"

"Your head, James. You hurt your head the other day."

"Ah, yes. Well, it's, er, better now."

"I'm glad." The wind roared in, and Montagu wrapped his cloak tight around himself.

"Don't have enough for the both of us, I'm afraid," Montagu said, following James's eyes.

"The other night!" James burst out.

"What about it, dear fellow?"

"You said—more time, coin," James spluttered, suddenly tired. Hallucinating was exhausting. He wasn't even sure why he sought answers any longer. The other night was different. For a moment, he had wondered if Montagu was someone he'd known, or ought to have known. Now, it did not seem to matter.

Montagu looked at him for a few moments, perplexed.

"Family. Fair hearing."

"Oh. I said all that, did I?"

"Yes."

Montagu rose and, with sprightly steps, began to pace the length of the cell. James backed away at the sudden movement, his alarm rising when Montagu crossed him. The demarcation of space, it seemed, had been abandoned.

"It's all very disturbing, you see," Montagu began, eyes darting around the cell, as though only vaguely aware of James's presence. "Very peculiar. Are you ready to listen?"

James glanced outside, almost hoping to see the guard.

"Well?" Montagu said, clicking his tongue.

James turned to him and nodded.

***

"I was always the unwanted child, the last son, the eyesore. My baron father was embarrassed to have me, the dunce who couldn't speak or walk for five years. The succession was safe, of course, but people would jeer. The doctors couldn't fix me, and the tutors couldn't teach me. By the time I came of age, I could barely write my name.

"My brilliant brothers—bless their souls—shielded me, took upon themselves the work of the estate, of riding and fighting and fucking, things that I could only dream of. I lived in luxury but remained uncomfortable, unable to bear the gaze of pity and loathing that I felt on my back.

"Slowly, painstakingly, hour by hour, day by day, I taught myself. Read reams and reams of paper. Studied till the night-lamps ran out of oil. Sacrificed my entire youth to catch up with the world, and finally, I developed my mind. Unworthy of marriage or responsibility, as I had been declared, my transformation went unnoticed. For a while, I was happy. But my life, it soon turned out, had become bereft of purpose.

"And then the dreams began. Of faraway lands, mountains ripping into the skies, bountiful red soil, rivers of gold and silver, cities fortified three times round, buildings awash with colour, stone sculptures of exquisite beauty, olive-skinned women wrapped in silk and satin, markets bursting with more riches than you could ever imagine.

"I could not forget them. I had read enough to know that such lands lay beyond the seas, and it became my duty to find them. Rich, competent, brilliant as they were—my brothers and even my wretched father—all lacked vision. Their world began and ended with our lands, our estate. But when I expressed a desire to tour even our own lands, I was laughed at, ridiculed. After all, what good was travel to a dunce?

"I waited. I plotted. I went to Mother; she refused me her aid. I sought some gold, which too was denied. And so, I sought out the merchants. They were sceptical at first—my reputation preceded me everywhere—but, unlike my family, they soon realised that I was no dullard. I spun them such visions of riches and treasure that the salivating fools were quickly eating out of my hands. A ship and some competent sailors were all I needed, and I would quit this accursed island forever.

"Alas, this proved my undoing. The life I'd led had given me little by way of experience. I chanced upon a sailor at a tavern in one of our villages. He promised the ship if I could produce the gold. Stumbling over myself in eagerness, I paid him part of the price. And never heard from him again.

"The creditors, having got wind of my dealings, began to snap at my heels. The gold I returned—their own—was a woeful amount. Though they'd entered into the contract with their eyes open, they soon branded me a lunatic, a madman who dreamt of invented lands and saw hidden treasure wherever he looked.

"My brilliant brothers finally stopped shielding me. The family gold, it was decided, did not belong to me—the unwanted son, the unfit son, the mad son. The merchants were baying for my blood. The final solution suited everyone. The merchants were given a nibble at the estate worth half their dues, while I was carted away to this godless town to live out my days in this hellish prison. With you, James."

***

Gasping for breath, Montagu—seeming to shrink again—trotted back to his corner. James knew that he ought to be quick with his words, lest Montagu slip out of this remarkable consciousness. But try as he might, he could only gape as Montagu sank to the floor and turned away.

Daylight had faded, and had taken the storm with it. Montagu's extraordinary revelations seemed to reverberate through the darkened cell, etch themselves in James's mind. It was no hallucination. James clamped his eyes shut and realised that he had lost Montagu for the night, possibly many nights, when he heard an even, peaceful breathing. He ought to be frustrated, frenzied, that one who had revealed himself to be so like him had slipped away with no assurance of return. But James, too, felt at peace.

It could not have been a hallucination. James knew himself—was sure that he, and even his deepest stream of consciousness, had a limited capacity for romance and fantasy. Montagu's story and the depth of his transient emotions—bitterness, pride, a naked, infinite ambition, and finally, a crippling despair—convinced James that his brain had not degenerated.

His peace, though, was more than just relief. Montagu had fallen silent, he felt, by design. Further conversation at that very moment would be of little use. He had said not a word to Montagu about the events leading up to his own incarceration. Montagu had not deemed it necessary to find that out as a condition to relating his own tale. Surely that was no accident. Surely Montagu would have withheld his past from someone he looked upon as a delinquent.

No, it was not just a madman's blabber. Montagu wanted, *needed,* his companion to ponder his words, his fate.

Their fate. James turned onto his side and fell asleep.

***

"What've you done to 'im?"

Montagu hadn't stirred in four days, save for the occasional mutters at night. *Gibberish,* James thought irritably. His patience was beginning to wear thin.

"If 'e dies in here, they'll have yer head."

"Or yours," James whispered to himself, turning towards Montagu.

"It gets to all of 'em soon. Took you longer than the rest, I'll give you that. But the *agony* of the gaol...." James blinked at the unexpected articulation. "It gets to yer," the guard said, his voice rising. "It gets to all of yer, thieving bastard!"

James sighed as the guard's stomps faded away and stood to use the privy. He cursed as he crossed Montagu's sleeping form, cursed the very fate that he had thanked in the aftermath of their extraordinary exchange for placing him in the vicinity of such high intellect, a man who would have remained beyond his reach but for the confines of this cell.

He squatted and groaned as his stomach ran. They were running out of sand. His stony pleas had met with an equal resistance from the guard. *He'll relent when the stench becomes unbearable,* James thought, as he wiped himself and rose.

What would return Montagu to sanity? Even for a few moments? How could he bring him back, move the conversation along? It was a conversation, he reassured himself for the umpteenth time. An unfinished conversation, one that was bound to compel them—victims of a similar misfortune—to discuss a reckoning.

Even though he harboured doubts about ventures so grandiose that they involved crossing the seas, James was convinced that Montagu was blessed with what he claimed his family lacked. A vision, the roots of which he had deigned to mention to James, a stranger. But one that would tie them all together; Montagu and James and the several others like them, and countless others to follow in the centuries to come.

Brave men—not on fields of needless slaughter and plunder—but those who laid empires of gold, bound, unlike the petty kingdoms of yesterday and tomorrow, to endure in perpetuity. James glanced at the window. Little drops of rain had begun to patter at the walls, a stray drizzle that would not last long. The crack in the ceiling started to leak once more.

"Raining again, then?"

James jerked his head in the direction of the faint whisper.

"Montagu!" He hissed, scrambling closer. "I mean, Sir. Mr—"

"Sir?" Montagu chuckled weakly. "I take it you haven't forgotten our last conversation. Has it been much time?"

"A few days," James panted.

"Forgive me. It takes me time to recover, you know. Sometimes, I don't know my own mind. But I remember," Montagu spoke aloud now, his voice hoarse but firm.

James felt his excitement rise, and after one last look at the guard's empty chair, he abandoned all inhibition.

"You said, you said, those merchants, your creditors, they—"

"I know what I said! But what's it to you?"

"Everything."

Montagu sighed and propped himself up against the wall. James drew closer.

"And why would you trust a raving lunatic, James?"

"I don't believe you are one."

"The rest of the world does, and those are the kinder ones."

"The likes of us can't afford to care about what others think!"

"Us?" Montagu raised an eyebrow.

"We must continue. The last time you spoke and then subsided into silence, but I've had little else to think of since then. The kind ones think of me as a merchant or a usurer—but I'm not! I'm not. I neither buy from one to sell to another, nor do I borrow from one to lend to another."

"Then what? What are you?"

James flinched at the hostility of the words.

"Well?"

"I—"

"And the rude ones?"

"What?"

"The kind ones say....But the unkind ones?"

"Cheat. Fraud. Thief. Fiend."

"They may well be right," Montagu sneered. James blinked and shifted away. "I have given offence."

"I thought we had something in common. Perhaps I was wrong."

"Common!" Montagu laughed. "Common is what you are, James. It is the most common of men who consider their petty lives the most uncommon."

Heaving, Montagu coughed and spat blood. It occurred to James that Montagu was probably afflicted with a physical disease, in addition to his other ailments. He watched closely as Montagu wiped his mouth with the sleeve of an unsteady hand. More was sure to come. If anything, the wanton insults had convinced him that Montagu's natural demeanour—natural for a man of high stature and pedigree—was revealing itself.

Montagu drew in a deep breath and shuddered. "I've heard of you, James."

"You have?"

"While I was doing my rounds, seeking credit." Montagu coughed again, bent double this time.

"The creditors, the merchants," Montagu continued hoarsely. "How was it a fair bargain to have me carted away here, wipe me from existence?"

"You're an unfortunate man. As am I."

"You're just a trader! Just an ugly brute from a small town, cursed with a small mind, unable to employ your own faculties. Unable to *think*."

"That's not true!" James's shrill protest bounced off the walls.

"What are you then? Flitting from one failed venture to another, is that what you're going to tell me? The carter at the village fair has more honour than the likes of you."

Montagu hawked and spat more blood.

"I don't *flit* from one venture to another." The even and slow words, quick on the heels of their heated exchange, made Montagu look up.

"I *am* the venture. And so, I am here, entrapped by my creditors. As for that matter, aren't you?"

The older man gaped. James met his gaze coolly, knowing that he had held his own.

"Then *think,*" Montagu hissed, holding his head in his hands. "*Think,* James, if you consider yourself my equal."

"I don't care about equality!"

Montagu laughed. "Two paupers in a prison cell, one of them on his deathbed, or death-stone, debating equality. The kingdom must be prospering."

"I don't care about bettering you. I have much to achieve outside. So many thoughts, plans that may be beyond even your grasp."

"Yet, you won't employ your mind," Montagu snapped. "I was asleep for days on end, but it seems I've considered our problems more than you have in all your time in this hell-hole."

James pursed his lips. "I don't know what you mean."

"But don't you see, James? All your ideas, plans, every last one of them is of no use if it can land you back in this hovel!"

"So, what do you mean? What have you considered? How can I employ my mind?"

"I don't have much time." James looked up. Montagu's eyes had slid out of focus, and he stared vacantly at the prison bars. "No time," Montagu whispered, gazing at the bars.

"Montagu! Mr Montagu!" James shouted, moving closer and grabbing the older man by the shoulders.

"My-name-is-Mr-Montagu-and-that-is-what-you-may-call-me," Montagu croaked.

"No, no, not yet! Mr Montagu!"

Montagu's pupils slid back into focus.

"The king is dead, James!" He gasped. "Long-live-the...king!"

With a deep, shuddering breath, Montagu slumped back, his head rolling against the stone behind him. James screamed and knelt, holding the older man by his bony shoulders and shaking him.

"What do you mean? Montagu! What do we think about?"

Montagu blinked.

"Hello, James. Is it raining?"

"No!"

"Get away from him!" Heavy steps thudded towards them.

Hunched over the older man, James felt a sudden current seize his frail body. Montagu began to convulse, rocking back and forth like a puppet in James's arms.

"Get away, for the *devil*, let him go! If yer kill him, they'll have our heads!" James could sense the guard's panic.

The convulsions stopped. James leaned in, smelt Montagu's sour breath.

"Mr Montagu."

Montagu's eyes flickered open. He gazed into James's eyes, but was focused on something far away.

"Unhand him, you bastard!" A jangle of the keys.

"Montagu. The king, the creditors..." James whispered.

"Yes. I will tell you, James, for want of a better heir to my legacy." He drew in a deep breath. "What we need, James. Is someone to stand between us and them."

"Who?"

"*Think*, James." Montagu's liquid brown eyes bored into James's as he heard the guard curse. "One who can borrow and expend without limit."

"But why would anyone—?"

"One," Montagu rasped, eyes gleaming, voice rising, "who can never be chased, James, nor chained! A formless power that cannot be seen, cannot be touched, cannot be killed, shrouded by a veil that cannot be lifted, capable of subjugating millions, and the millions to come after them!"

Montagu coughed. Spit and blood dribbled down his chin, onto his cloak. The key turned in the lock.

"The puppet when you seek the gold," he panted. "And the puppeteer, upon a default."

James stared.

"Not a he," Montagu spat out, beginning to convulse again. The bars clanged, and heavy boots pounded in. "Nor a she, James," he panted, as James leaned in to catch the fading words. "An *it*..."

Montagu drew in a sharp, heaving breath and fell back in a heap. James felt the guard lift him by his collar and toss him away. He landed on his elbows and knees and watched with a casual interest as the guard crouched over the most uncommon man whose company he had had the fortune to keep.

"He's *dead*!" The guard bellowed, turning to face James, his face white. "He's dead, an' *you* killed him." The guard began to wail, rocking on his feet.

James huddled in his corner and drew his knees up to his chest.

"The unseen companion," James said, marvelling to himself over the guard's hysterics. "Perpetual succession. An imperturbable veil." He rubbed his elbows absently. They were bleeding.

"Companie," James whispered to himself. Watching the guard gather up Montagu's lifeless body, James began to chuckle.

Gora

I still remember the day I got my uniform. Personally, I've never quite enjoyed the colour. It's what I imagine each speck of dust looks like. But I like the word. *Khaki.* It is exotic, foreign, a promise of prestige, if not wealth. I come from a family that has never tasted much of either. Maaji—the same Maaji who had refused to speak to me the day I had first announced my intention—could barely contain her pride. Pitaji, lips pursed, did not say much. But Maaji told me the next day that she had seen some moisture on the pillow, and could scarcely believe it herself. The village—otherwise placid, hot, sleepy—was abuzz with the news.

Have you seen him in uniform?

Has he always been that tall?

Bloody stooge.

They'll kill him too, just the way they killed those young boys, across the black water.

After I first stepped into uniform, I began to dream of my commission. The stories were frightening. I was terrified of dying alone in some foreign land, entombed in ice and snow. But that was over. Bittu from the teashop told me one day that the war was over for good and everything was calm. The agitators had sprung up again, but what did that have to do with me? I could be just what I wanted—a proud *fauji* in my own land, with no unknown *gora* foes abroad. Nevertheless, I was stepping out of my village for the first time.

It's so far away! Do you even understand a word of the language? What'll you eat?

I had never met anyone as impressive as General-saab. He insisted that we call him by name. I suppose it was meant to imbibe a sense of familiarity. But now, more than ever, I will call him General-saab.

Subedaar! You will call me General. You can also call me General Reginald. But none of this saab nonsense. Do you understand me?

That clipped accent. The click of those boots. The dismissive manner. Authority came naturally to him. It seemed like General-saab had never had to answer to anyone in his whole life. We didn't understand half the things he said. We were in awe.

At the barracks, my new companions were Parihar, a stout Rajput, and Thapa, a Gorkha. I'd seen Rajputs before, had heard of their love for camels. But I'd never met someone like Thapa. He came from 2,000 kilometres away, whatever that meant. He'd grown up in villages carved out of dense jungle, and his people were a hardy lot. Once the Saabs discovered that, they wasted no time in making a regiment out of them. So, unlike me, he came from an established military pedigree. He'd always known that he'd join the army. Even Parihar had some distant relatives who'd dabbled in service.

Thankfully, we received our commissions this year. A few months back, we'd be rotting in some trench, blood and bones frozen.

My uncle was killed, just like that, in France.

Where is France?

Near England.

That doesn't help.

It's all I know.

So, what were we to do then? I thought we were just meant to strut around, rifles on our shoulders. It was my first time in a city. I had never seen so many people in one go. It made me dizzy, even though Thapa told me that there were even larger cities down south.

General-saab drove us hard. There was never enough food, never enough sleep. But we were happy. It was a new world, a new life. People lowered their eyes when they spotted us marching along. It was a heady feeling.

The real heady feeling, though, came on the day that I learnt to shoot a gun. I had never even gotten close to one before. Everyone in the village placed their faith in thick, knobbly sticks that did the job just as well. But when I first held the gleaming Lee-Enfield in my hand, intoxicated by the scent of polish, blinded by the shining steel of the bayonet, I felt light-headed. The gun was heavy. Thapa knew all about them already and had assured us that he'd help us keep up. We had to shoot in groups of four. It was one of those rare days that General-saab came to watch us practice.

Thapa was part of one of the first groups. I watched with envy as he, with effortless grace, mounted the machine onto his shoulder, took aim and fired. He did not hit the target, but his aim was stellar. As he walked back, smelling of gunpowder, forehead shining with sweat, he grinned at us.

Parihar was in the next group. The giant lad was clumsy, and his shooting was all over the place. Much like I expected mine to be, so I nodded at him in sympathy as he returned to position, downcast. My palms grew clammy as I walked up to the mark. Out of the corner of my eye, I could see General-saab watching with bored eyes, which somehow brought on a rush of confidence. Taking a deep breath, I placed the butt firmly on my shoulder, held still and took careful aim.

I can't believe you've never shot before! You're a liar.

Three shots on target! It made General-saab sit up.

You definitely have some army blood in your veins, you lying bastard.

I cannot gather the exact memory of that moment. It eludes me like the squiggle before your eyes—it follows you everywhere you look, but if you try to focus, it quivers and takes flight. Only flashes come to mind. The acrid smell of smoke. The punch of the recoil on my shoulder. The sound of the bullet—my bullet—hitting the wall, and of my own breath, amplified in between shots. But try as I might, I cannot recall the exact moment when I pulled the trigger. I reach for it, grab at it, flail against it. But it evades me.

Bang.

Bang.

Bang.

The novelty of it all soon seeped away. We settled into a routine. Of all our tasks, we enjoyed patrol duty the most. At the barracks, even though we were kept on our feet from morning till night, it quickly became drab. The teeming city, however, never ceased to amaze.

We heard the rumours, the grumblings. But just like everyone else at the barracks, we ignored them. In the army, we were taught to toe the line. And General-saab tore into anyone who so much as whispered about the goings-on in the city. We took the hint.

Have you heard? It's called the Rowl—

Shhh. Everyone's heard, but if General-saab...

Relax, it's just a big joke anyway. Who cares if people are detained? Why don't they just mind their business peacefully, and General-saab will leave them alone. He's not an evil man, you know.

Parihar was the excitable one; he enjoyed gossiping. Thapa had lineage to worry about, so he kept his own counsel. And me? I was terrified of General-saab. The mere thought of being stripped of my uniform and turning back to my village, banished in disgrace, made me shiver.

We could ignore what we heard, but can the eyes ever forget what they've seen? Sticky with syrup, our fingers teased the *jalebis,* trying to cool them by breaking them into smaller pieces. I heard the cries just as I was biting into a juicy morsel.

Crawl, you mongrel.

Mercy, please, mercy.

You dare besmirch this spot? English blood not yet dry…

Mercy, mercy…

We never finished our *jalebis* that day. The memory of Major Smith's contorted face, teeth bared, eyes spewing hate, was enough to rob us of our appetite. General-saab's visits to the barracks became more frequent. Each time, he looked more agitated than the last. At times, during shooting practice, I caught him gazing at us, his expression inscrutable, a slight curl of the lip betraying his mind.

With each passing day, the unrest of the city threatened to breach the stout walls of the barracks. General-saab restricted patrol duty to the *goras* in the regiment. With them gone, there was less work at the barracks. We were often left twiddling our thumbs for hours on end. The rumours filtered in unbidden, probing at our little bubble, arousing our curiosity.

I've heard that lakhs go to listen to him speak.

What's he done, anyway?

Some funny business in Champaran. The goras are scrambling. General-saab looks like thunder these days.

That day dawned like any other. We hadn't been to the city in three weeks. But that day, General-saab wanted us ready at 3. We stood in the yard, perspiring in the afternoon sun, rifles held erect by our sides. Two armoured cars stood by the gate. General-saab said little, tugging at his moustache. The orders were simple.

It was a large gathering, but the park was surprisingly quiet. A sonorous voice filtered through the sole entrance. Though we were barely 90 men, the clamour of our boots against the road was reminiscent of the charge of cavalry.

Clip-clop, clip-clop.

The elephants were too large to fit through the entrance. They came rolling to a stop. The narrow passageway had space for only two men, shoulder to shoulder. Parihar and I fell into step. I bid the fleeting darkness to go on forever, for this tunnel to elongate and swallow us into the bosom of the earth. Sunlight streamed through too soon. Heads turned as we marched in.

Clip-clop, clip-clop.

What was most striking about the park was the peace. People stretched as far as the eye could see. Standing, squatting, sitting, leaning. People of every kind. Yet, there was peace. They listened in silence as the man spoke on. Heads turned to look at us, and then turned back.

The cavalry in, the commander swaggered in last. His eyes, bloodshot, like a drunk's, gleamed with colonial fervour. Legs apart, he stood behind our columns, his *khaki* crisp and striking in the soft sunlight.

A recalcitrant child escaped his mother's grasp and turned to stare at us. A beautiful child, hair curly and eyes bright.

The orders were simple.

Subedaaaars! Ready!

The butt nestled into my shoulder, into the cosy nook it had carved out for itself over the past few months. I looked straight ahead, through eyes that had glazed over, at nothing in particular. Cries rent the air. Birds took flight. Orderly no more, the crowd began to scatter. I could not see the beautiful child.

Aim!

I inhaled the polish. It smelled sweet, but rancid at the same time. I should have polished it some more. Target practice had carved a horizontal sore into the top of my index finger. The sore now greeted the trigger like an old friend. Some of the crowds were jumping over the wall. It was too high. A few rushed towards the well at the centre of the park. I spotted the beautiful child in his mother's arms as she made for the well.

FIRE!

Bang.

Bang.

Bang.

My countrymen screamed. I silenced them. I was the best shot in the barracks.

Ready. Aim. Fire. Ready. Aim. Fire. Ready. Aim. Fire.

Reload.

Ready. Aim. Fire.

We never spoke of that day. We never even acknowledged it. Parihar soon got transferred. Thapa too rose in the ranks and made his way closer to home. I stay on in Amritsar, under General-saab's watchful eye.

The barracks are quiet. My comrades are asleep. I am a stranger to sleep. I look down at my fingers. They tremble slightly. I have always been fair. But today, my skin shines white. *Gora.*

My service rifle beckons. The barrel is smooth—the bayonet glints. Tonight, I don't need to be the best shot in the barracks.

Skin

When I was a boy, my father had to choose. Heart or mind. Tradition or modernity. Faith or peace.

"Why did you run?" The man rasped, taking his time to catch his breath. For an elderly man, he was sprightly, a fact he reminded his acolytes of as they caught up. Four in all. They slapped each other's backs, as a relay team might at the end of a successful race.

I felt the bricks behind me—solid, immutable, unyielding—and cursed them for arresting my flight.

"Why?" He repeated with a quizzical half-smile. The others stood back in deference to their leader, gathered in a loose arc.

The afternoon sunlight danced off their blades. Metal clanged in the distance. Glass shattered. Lazy laughter, pierced by muffled screams, rent the air. I heard the patter of feet in parallel lanes, smelled the sour breath of sweating men and the iron of blood.

The leader grinned. I averted my eyes and looked at the shuttered shops for someone, something, anything.

"Maybe he's a mute," an acolyte with a scar across his face drawled. "Even for them, that's quite heartless, to leave their disabled out as easy meat…"

Instinctively, they turned in the direction of a resounding boom not too far away. A gas cylinder, perhaps. Or a car.

"But he's certainly not deaf," the leader said, seeing me flinch.

"Name? What's your name?" The youngest, a stripling of a boy, bellowed as if to test scar-face's theory.

"We are *pissing away* precious time," snarled the man with the saffron scarf. "The DSP said he could only delay his men till 4, and it's nearly 3…" The sound of a gunshot pierced the silence of the lane. Saffron scarf bared sharp, yellowing teeth that accentuated the glower of his eyes. "The others seem to be making steady progress while we debate with some mute son of a bitch."

"Quiet!" The leader snapped. "Don't forget that we lost three young men last time because of your misplaced fervour."

Saffron scarf looked mutinous, but he held his tongue.

"So, tell us, boy," the leader said, stepping closer. "You have one chance… Consider yourself lucky. At least we ask." He smiled at me as one might at a neighbour. He was not unpleasant-looking: portly, with a thin, greying moustache and thick glasses that gave him the air of a schoolmaster. My frenzied brain conjured up an image of him instructing young boys, ruling over them with a benign but firm hand.

"What made you run?" He rasped. "You seem to be from a good family, western clothes and all."

"Which would make it even better," Saffron scarf said, licking his lips and surveying me with distaste.

My arm, trembling and useless by my side, pinched my jeans. My father had always insisted that we wear the most modern clothes, the trendiest brands we could afford, even on the most familial of occasions.

Springing forward with surprising agility, the leader caught me by the jaw. "Smooth chin," he breathed. A single grain of rice stuck to the vermillion on his forehead broke free and fell to the ground. "No cap-ring on his head either," he said, running a gnarled hand over my hair. And yet…" he said, holding me by the chin, between thumb and forefinger. "We sent word out for men, but you did not come. We sent word to the cowards to stay home, hide behind their mothers' *pallus*. Yet, you roam free… here. With impunity."

Tilting my face, he ran an elegant finger over my cheek. "And you ran," he whispered. I caught a whiff of fennel on his breath, the palate cleanser after a meal, perhaps, before they had set out. "You ran," he repeated, eyes boring into my soul, reaching for the taint he had been taught to pursue.

Blood pounded in my temples, threatening to breach the dam of my skull and burst forth. Vision blurring, I tried to focus on the whites of his eyes.

His face cleared, then contorted in a manic grin. "He's yours," he barked at the youngest of the lot, releasing me with a jerk and stepping back to join them. The young chap crowed and stepped forward, grabbing saffron scarf's sword on the way.

I fought off your mother, grandfather, and the clerics for this, beta. It is a small sacrifice, but... times are bad. When the time comes... use it.

Blade in the air, eyes bloodshot, muscles rippling, the chap swaggered up.

"Watch out! Sometimes they fight back!" The leader called out with childish glee.

Use it, said the voice in my head. *Use it...NOW.*

Eyes glued shut, I raised a hand to shield myself from the impending attack. With the other, I reached for my trousers.

"And what the fuck is this?"

I opened my eyes. The rust of the blade was inches from my neck. The youth stood before me, statuesque, disgust moulding his boyish features into an ugly grimace.

"He's going to fight you with that toothpick," scar-face chortled.

"You fucking pervert!" The youth raised a hand to strike.

"Wait."

The men followed their leader's gaze to my midriff, to stare at the tiny strip of skin that had made its presence felt in the deserted alley like an unwelcome guest.

The blade dropped to the boy's side. He trotted back with the downcast air of one who has been denied a sumptuous feast.

"Let's go," the leader said, his voice curt. "The others need us."

"Shouldn't he join us, then?" Saffron scarf's voice was thick with disappointment.

"This scrawny fellow?" Scar-face jeered. "No, let's leave him to roam the streets and brandish that at whoever he pleases. Even my youngest brother—"

"Next time," the leader said, cutting him off and addressing me in a measured tone, "do as a coward does, and stay home."

The young chap kicked the air as they retraced their steps down the lane. "Fucking ill luck. Set out to serve your community, and one of them waves that in your face." He hawked and spat in the gutter. Saffron scarf sniggered.

The leader laughed and patted the boy's shoulder. "Patience, my young friend, patience... Let's try the next lane."

The lane was clear, and my eyes brought the ground together in sharp focus. I looked past my flaccid saviour, watched the urine pool at my feet, spatter my jeans, its intermittent patter mingling with the harsh gasps of my breath.

When I was a boy, my father had to choose. Heart or mind. Tradition or modernity. Faith or peace. Life, or death.

Second Flight

The train chugs into Kanchipuram station. A thousand kilometres from home, from him. And five hundred away from Tirunelveli, from the village.

He was perplexed when I asked to come, more so when I insisted on taking the train, and downright agitated when I demanded that I come alone. It was not like him to refuse—it was less like me to ask, to demand. We never speak of the village. He probed a little, extended a cautious foot into the pool whose depths I had never cared to define.

"Whose wedding? How close are you—we—to them? Why not fly?"

"I get airsick," I said.

"We've flown before," he countered, a quiver in his voice. I hated him then, hated the veiled accusation, the guilty concern.

"It's easier to sleep," I said. And think, I didn't say. He shook his head and booked my ticket.

"You're blessed," say my friends, wizened, old, unencumbered. "The planets have conspired to trap you with such a gentle soul."

Not trap. I can't think of an appropriate substitute. It's everything and nothing. Every day and never. Ever since the wheels of my frenetic life came to a grinding halt, with my retirement as Head Librarian of Lokhande Memorial Municipal School, one hundred and ninety-five days ago, I've been like this.

I watch a family of five laugh as they struggle to load too many suitcases through the tiny door. The father, tall and dark, forehead shining with sweat under the late evening sun, directs proceedings, curling one end of his bushy moustache. The traditional dress, white cotton shirt, cream *veshti*, gold-bordered *angavastram*, and the authoritative manner bring Him to mind.

What did I expect?

"Do you ever think of Him?" Sudha asked me a few evenings ago, after an enervating hour of pretend piety at the neighbourhood *kovil*.

"I can't remember," I replied unbidden then, though it bothers me still. Can't I remember Him? Can I simply not remember thinking of Him? I feel no guilt. He was no more than a passing acquaintance, a friend who asked—and received—everything, and vanished before giving back. And after all, Sridhar looks nothing like Him.

I watch the father bring in the last of the luggage, biceps flexing with the effort. Admiring his sturdy arms, I recall a brown, hairy pair from another life, which exulted in the ease with which they swept me off the ground.

Twenty-seven years ago, I ran. His family asked—or proposed, as they liked to say—that I go, even as His pyre cooled. That I swap the green hills for the grey city across the mainland and build an alien life for myself. And so, clutching my swollen belly, cursing my poor, weak brother for not standing up to them, huddled ticketless in a passenger train hurtling across the peninsula in the opposite direction, I fled, vowing never to return.

The family troops in, luggage colliding against every surface in sight. Pointing at the berths around me, the children announce the discovery of their seats. I sigh and eye the three of them, two girls and a boy—brown, gleeful, cackling balls of energy. They plonk themselves on the berth across me, sitting in a line like crows on a wire, each turning their expectant gaze upon me. I say nothing.

"There's a *patti* here!" The more petite girl, no more than four, exclaims. There is no grandchild to call me so.

The parents, having located their other berths in the next bay, return and make a half-hearted attempt to shush the children.

The father hangs back. "Sorry, *mami,*" the mother says, with a half-apologetic smile, no doubt banking on the assumption of shared maternal sentiment for me to smile back and comment on the loveliness of the children, and of children in general, and wave an understanding hand, and no, of course they aren't a nuisance.

"I'm not too well," I say. The children pause their games to absorb this utterance, promptly resuming their play once it fades into nothingness.

"Yes, er…" The mother flashes a strained smile and addresses her husband in short, irritable bursts of anglicised Tamil. I follow every word—he is ordered to deal with me, and the mother needs rest in preparation for an exhausting wedding. I turn on my side, away from the unwelcome hullabaloo of the compartment.

Twenty-seven years. I stare at the blue-dotted pattern on the wall of the compartment. The price of a new life. The reinvention of Savitri. Does anyone have twenty-seven years to spare? Did I have them?

I wasn't always this calculative. There is no scale on which to weigh the life that's fallen in your lap, Neelima used to say in the initial days in that tiny one-bedroom flat, stroking my hair as I cried rivers of rage and sorrow. Words I learnt to live by. And did live by.

I spent the currency of my years, one by one. My son was born. His family paid the expenses. I needed a house. His family paid the rent. I needed a companion, some help. His family deposited Neelima, another runaway from the village—a willing one to boot, in my flat. Poor Neelima. Took her own advice and waltzed through life, but died still pining in silence after the man for whom she'd staked all.

Neelima. Sometimes, I still talk to her, seek her out on matters beyond my ken. The matronly housewife who stabilised my household. Cajoled me into venturing out in search of work, even as we sustained ourselves on His family's grudging charity.

Despite my broken Marathi, I finally managed an appointment as the Junior Assistant Librarian of Lokhande Memorial Municipal School, tasked with cataloguing endless piles of books that no pupil would ever borrow, nor would I myself read.

Savitri-Amma, Head Librarian, Neelima liked to sing to Sridhar, who would shriek and giggle in response, then look at me with those beseeching eyes, seeking an answering song. "Why do you never sing to him?" Neelima asked at times, pleading with me in an almost wifely fashion. I avoided the question with manly agility each time.

They withdrew the charity a few months into my appointment, the airy twin assumptions that they'd done enough and that I had enough, never uttered, but made nonetheless. Perhaps Neelima told on me. I often think that she was their mole. We never did get around to talking about that. But who was I to say anything when she brought up my son as a mother should?

Invitations from the village—to weddings, thread ceremonies, *arangetrams*—trickled in dutifully, informed me in shrill colours of the prosperity of their senders. Some censor with a keen eye must have withheld the annual *katcheri* invitation. I never understood why they bothered.

They pricked me in the initial years, those invitations. When I still had Neelima, and some time to brood over a life that had slipped beyond reach and recognition. But time passed. Memory faded. I got word that my brother had drunk himself to death. Neelima passed away without ceremony one night.

Sridhar, a chubby, boisterous toddler, grew into a skinny, quiet, astute teenager who divined that education was his only key to a different world. And so, burying himself in his studies, he plotted his escape from the accident of birth, even as I gave in absolutely to it. "If you survive, Neelima said to me on one of her last days, "even if you only survive this fight, it will be enough."

I couldn't understand her sometimes, but on that day, I had no interjection to offer. My tears had long dried. The embers of my anger, too, had cooled, lulled into extinguishment by the tedium of living. "Dreams are for those fashioned from milk, honey, and good fortune," she went on—an uncharacteristic addition, as if keen to illumine my path for life after her. "Dogged, unremarkable survival itself is victory for the rest. You'll remember that, won't you, Saavi?" I only nodded.

A scuffle and a slap. The youngest child bursts into tears. Her wails bring the mother rushing in. I turn back towards them to watch. The boy accepts his scolding with grace, even apologising without much prompting as the mother cuddles his sobbing sister. A few moments, hugs, and kisses later, the girl calms down. Satisfied with the truce and avoiding my eye, the mother leaves.

When your only goal is to endure, it can leave little room for affection. Maybe I was unfair to the boy. But families have their flaws. This was ours. It was unsaid and understood. To his credit, Sridhar discharged his part of the contract perfectly—nose always buried in a textbook, incurious about the past, never straying into trouble.

What I lacked in affection, I made up for with action, ensuring that we never lacked anything essential. We—and I—never had to supplicate before anyone. Neighbours who, after Neelima's passing, came around to offer their help were turned away with a polite smile and firm hand, as were the few louts in the neighbourhood who considered me easy game.

Right by Sridhar, and right by myself. Such platitudes, oft-repeated to myself, kept us going. But we had our joys too, as families do. My promotions and the increasing salaries that came with them, right up to Head Librarian. Sridhar's stellar performance in X, then XII, then the engineering entrance. The luxury of hiring a maid to cook and clean for us. Even affection began to flow between us with more freedom, as if it were shedding the burden of a tougher past, and urging us to do so, too.

At the farewell party six months ago, marking our escape from that tiny first flat, the neighbours and friends I had finally allowed in remarked that I was a great mother. They had gathered my story in bits and pieces, I suppose, none knowing the whole, but each enough to venture that this was a fitting occasion to make such a remark.

A great mother, an indomitable woman, a woman of substance. To have triumphed over such adversity, over this forbidding city that swallows most migrants whole without so much as a belch to acknowledge their existence.

Sridhar nodded and smiled at those who congratulated him for my saintliness, even joined in in the adulatory, one-way chorus, though he knew that we were equal partners in getting here, in being able to have a farewell party at all; swap our depressing one-room apartment for a spacious house with two bedrooms and a large bathroom, paid for by a job he had earned through single-minded pursuit of excellence at university, paid for by a government scholarship earned through single-minded pursuit of excellence at Lokhande Memorial Municipal School, paid for by my having been Junior Assistant/Assistant/Senior Assistant/Head Librarian.

I admit—I basked in the warm glow of their applause, even allowed myself to feel the weightless joy of happiness. I did it, I whispered to myself later that same night, as I staggered into my tiny bed for the last time. The village green, never too far from my thoughts and always an alluring emerald until that moment, turned pale and mouldy. The hue of my own life transformed from its customary dull grey and flashed a brilliant pink-gold.

I retired soon after that farewell party, handed over the responsibility for our well-being to the ever-dutiful Sridhar, so wedded to his work and to me that he showed no signs of wanting to become a householder in his own right. A rest, twenty-seven years after my flight.

The dark hills of the Eastern Ghats, jagged and irregular, flash past. Train attendants begin to weave between the berths, announcing the evening meal in practised, mechanical tones. I sit up, recalling the packet of fruit Sridhar had thrust into my hands at the last moment. The mother returns, clutching three steel tiffins, and proceeds to distribute neat food packets to the children.

Yes, I was happy that day. And it was a complete, round, neat happiness, well-earned and well-deserved. But now I've come undone. An insidious ennui has taken root in the fallow field of my mind, taunting me into retracing my steps after all this time. When do you know that you have fully discharged your purpose on earth?

Presumably, I ought to have known on the day of that farewell party. And I thought I did. Why, I even retired in the expectation of cornering that feeling, the one that might allow a once-struggling alien widow the pleasing aimlessness to cajole her prosperous, devoted son into bringing home a shy bride and shower free-flowing love on the grandchildren they beget.

I was wrong. For one who had never harboured any goals of her own making, how could I have predicted the cloying discomfort of a life without the anchor of a goal to weigh it down?

I lost all interest in that new plush life for which I'd toiled the whole of my old one. The ennui, unwelcome and unsettling, shadowed me as I paced the rooms of our new house, its freshly painted walls smooth, shiny and oppressive. So too, I lost interest in Sridhar's ascendant life of wealth and excitement.

I heard him talk of the incessant travel and unexpected perks, watched him blossom into a more confident young man, all with the casual regard one reserves for one's second-favourite soap opera character.

Yet, I resisted. Tried to fill my days. Befriended some other retirees and maddeningly content housewives who shuffled around our pleasant new colony. Accepted each of their invitations to congregate to watch Tirupati *poojai* on television, accompanied them on their daily jaunt to the neighbourhood *kovil*, and sat still as they prostrated before their deity of choice, muttering prayers of gratitude and hope.

None lost the opportunity to gush about their heyday, and each spoke by turn with pride of their own achievements or the accolades earned by their husbands or children. Some even tried to fill the void of my silence by praising Sridhar and my stellar, single-handed upbringing of him.

I aped their actions, but I could not ape the glow of fulfilment that emanated from their souls. I took to acknowledging their kudos with quiet, expressionless smiles, the act suspended between a humble acceptance of it and a firm dissociation from the life that warranted it.

"It's just the nature of retirement, Amma." Sridhar smiled when I tried to confide in him. "You've done so much. It's my turn." His indulgence was kindling for the flames of resentment that had sprouted in my mind.

Neelima would have been shocked and indignant at my ingratitude. "You should thank God," she would hiss. "You came here with nothing. Look at you now! A queen in your son's palace, free to do as you please."

Are you free? Have you ever been? Will you ever be?

Such were some of the unanswerable questions the ennui posed as it mocked my placebo existence. I, who had lived by and almost relished the rigour of routine for so many years, found myself seeking out anything out of the ordinary, something to withdraw me noiselessly from the invisible turmoil that ebbed and flowed in my mind.

And then, the grand-niece's wedding invitation, forwarded to me by the conscientious new tenants of my old flat. The village. The one door whose key I had always held close to my breast—inaccessible to the few whom I counted among my loved ones, even to myself. The ennui—unforgiving, tenacious, insistent, probing—crowed as I rang the shocked niece; purred when I, with uncharacteristic speed, confronted Sridhar and arranged for my travel.

The train wheezes to a halt. No station is in sight. The black hills stand stolid in the distance, appearing to embrace under the weak moon.

But why, I ask of the ennui again. Why did you taunt me into breaking my vow, when there is nothing for me in the village, nor anything once I return home? It maintains the studied silence it had lapsed into at Mumbai Central.

The unscheduled halt lengthens. Fellow passengers, lulled into sleep by the train's rhythmic sway, begin to stir. Some check their watches with groggy eyes and call for the ticket collector. The mother sits across from me, stroking the forehead of her fussing youngest. The elder ones are asleep, curled up in their respective berths. I peel and eat a banana.

The ticket collector arrives, panting. "A puzzling spark in the engine," he informs the now-worried passengers who gather around him, the mother included. "No fire, no need to panic. But the train stays here until we determine the cause and deem it fit to carry on. Try and get some sleep," he finishes, before hurrying off. People mutter but withdraw to their berths.

Am I a fool to turn this way? Would a pilgrimage not suffice to break the monotony?

The child, visibly exhausted, scowls and wails.

"Mami, can I dim the lights?" The mother asks. I nod.

I watch as she sits back and draws the fussing child's head onto her lap with tender hands. Bending towards her as if to block out all the noise of the world, she begins to sing. Rigid and upright in my berth, I gaze out at the still, ethereal, silver landscape. The lilting melody floats up to me. It carries a mother's love, but not a singer's skill.

I can never forget this song. I shut my eyes, sift through my memory to place the film. Its name evades me playfully for a moment, then reveals itself. *Pasamalar*. An old film even for Him and me. I follow the words as the mother sings on. I can picture it in my mind's eye. The images flash past; fresh, clear, colourful.

My namesake, Savitri, eyeing a swaddled infant lovingly before she picks her up and croons to her. Sivaji Ganesan, an early heartthrob, does the same in a shakier voice with a baby boy. The mother draws a breath and begins again. I mouth the words along with her.

Other images and sensations, older than that fateful flight that I am recreating in reverse, suppressed until now with fury and determination, force their way through, unsolicited. The ennui steps back in silence, but sharpens them into focus.

The throngs at the village *katcheri* who flocked to hear me sing. My stolen glances at His face, eyes closed, relishing the ecstasy of my voice. My brother's croak of shock when He came to seek my hand. The buzz of whispers that tailed me afterwards—the share-cropper's fatherless daughter, the seductress of the zamindar's most beautiful son.

His taste, his scent, his breath, on that first night of frenzied lovemaking. I broke into this song that night, an unconscious choice, as He lay panting, our legs intertwined. "Sing this to our children," He said when I paused, drawing me close with those iron arms. I giggled and went on.

"You'll be a sensation in Madras," he said. "I'll make you one. I'll take you there. The crowds at the *katcheri* here are puddles compared to the ocean of people you'll enchant in the city. Just don't stop singing for me."

I sang Him other songs. But I ended each night with this one. Madras was never far from his lips. "After Sridhar is born," he said when I finished, on the night that He stopped breathing.

I have never gone to Madras.

They stole from me. All of them. He, by falling in love with me, by loving my voice, by embracing the cool abyss of death before bringing those loves to fruition. They, by forsaking me without a second glance, denying me even the sweet punishment due to a zamindar's widow.

My incoherent brother, by abandoning my side in my hour of need. Sridhar, by inhabiting my womb, taking birth as my son, thrusting on me the gratuitous, exacting, immutable goal of survival. And finally, Neelima, my guardian, companion, sister, by denying me my right to dream.

"Amma, are you okay?" The mother asks. I open my eyes to her concerned gaze and sense the tears streaming down my cheeks. I lift a hand to wipe them.

"Yes," I say. The child babbles, happier than before, but still awake. I gesture at her. "Can I try?"

The mother is surprised, but too tired to engage. "Of course, Amma."

I, too, am surprised. I haven't sung since that night. I take a deep breath and begin the song. Vivid in my mind until a few moments ago, His face fades, flickers, and then slides out. The child quietens. The mother heaves a sigh and shuts her eyes. I, too, close mine. My voice is light as it floats through the bittersweet melody.

The ennui lifts as my voice strengthens. My mind empties, but for the images of the song. I can picture my namesake actress again, smiling and cooing at an infant. I can see the infant, too, but it is different from the one in the film. It smiles. It is not Sridhar, either.

It is you, the ennui says, breaking its silence as it dissipates. Just Savitri.

I finish the song and open my eyes. The girl is fast asleep, thumb in her mouth. The mother stirs, splutters out a weak thanks, and slumps back onto the seat, soon emitting quiet snores.

The train remains still. The carriage is abuzz with the grumbling of irate passengers. I rise, cross the aisle with light steps, pull open the door ahead of the last berth, and step onto the landing. The carriage door is open and unmanned. I stand at the top step and grasp the handrail. Staring out at the vast, open countryside bathed in the pale light of the waning moon, I recall a conversation with Neelima on a night train to Shirdi, a mewling Sridhar perched on her lap.

"What would you do if you found yourself out there?" I'd asked, pointing to the rugged land that flashed past, laughing when she shivered at the thought.

"I'd sit cross-legged, right by the railway tracks, and wait for the next train to come take me home," she'd said. "You?"

"I'd turn around and walk into the hills."

Smiling, unseen and alone, I step off the train and begin to walk. Just Savitri. I can see the lights of a village flickering in the distance.

The Perfect Cut

I

"This simply won't do, boy."

Boy. Even Appa, usually unfazed, looked worried.

"Just *how*—" Thatha spluttered, continuing to scowl at the examination paper in his hand, as though the offending numbers would slide right off, to be meekly replaced by ones respectable enough to boast about to the aunties at the temple office he had come to run. I wondered why he was so bothered.

He invariably inflated them by 5%, sometimes 10% if in a particularly jolly mood. It was faintly amusing that he seemed to need some semblance of truth about them; that it seemed a moral offence against Shanthi Mami and Pillai Uncle to have to exaggerate beyond a customary threshold.

The first time, it was a fluke. Being some minor test or another, it never came to anyone's attention. After all, I was well past the age when every little fact and event of my life was to be exclaimed about. It was only towards September, that no-good, characterless month, that my replies could no longer remain vague.

The usual questions about my exam prep, jokes about the neighbour's son (bloody smug, bespectacled, genius of a Shankar), and rising interest in my general existence uncovered some rather unpalatable truths about my mathematical acumen.

Appa finally broke his silence. "But what *happened*?"

We stared at the sheet, finally at rest on the dining table. 56.75. Scrawled in big red digits, enclosed in an ellipsis. Like a sleeping egg. The teacher's careless pen had left the ends of the egg poking out, crossing each other. I only mention this because in one of the questions, something about the calculation of the something of a bridge, against my sketch of the bridge (a couple of sagging lines, no doubt weighed down by my ignorance and atrocious drawing skills), along with an angry zero, she'd taken care to remark, *What kind of bridge is this*?

"We've never interfered with you much, but—"

"And it was a colossal mistake," Thatha muttered, with a cough that sounded suspiciously like *Shankar*.

Bloody bastard. Probably beat me by 40 marks.

"But this seems to be cause for concern," Appa finished.

There were many things I wished for as a child. Curly hair. The Mewtwo Pokémon card. A crackling backhand like Justine Henin. The ability to unerringly *solve for x*, however, was not one of them.

"Dei, tell us, da," Thatha adopted a low tone, trying and failing to sound comforting.

I conjured up a downcast expression and stared at my feet. One of the hairs on the large toe of my left foot had grown to a noteworthy length. To be honest, though I sympathised with their outrage, I had no words to offer, in my defence or otherwise.

It had just slipped away one day, sidled out of my life like a disgruntled lover, taking with it a multitude of memories that now felt foreign—the scholarship certificate (first standard), selection for the maths Olympiad (fourth standard), countless top test results. There were the odd slippages here and there as I progressed, but nothing outside the ordinary. I always pulled through in the end. A stellar show in the ninth standard end term (91; Shankar: 96), and things seemed on track as ever.

Until this moment.

"Well, I never thought this day would come, but," Thatha sighed. I looked up, more out of curiosity than anything else. "You need a tutor, boy." He exhaled these words, breaking it to me as one would the news of an incurable affliction.

My throat tightened. Instantly, I thought of an evil, moustachioed character, a frustrated, underpaid schoolteacher whose favourite hobby was shouting at teenagers after hours. This, I had not bargained for. Even as I felt my mathematical ability recede, I had rather hoped that I would ultimately breeze through, pull it off like I had in the past, without darkening some tutor's doors, or him darkening mine. I glared at my answer sheet. My breezing days seemed over.

"We should've done this a long time ago," Thatha barked at Appa, beginning to pace the room. Always a bad sign. "Put him in one of those advanced learning classes. Sumathi put her daughter in one, and she's only in seventh standard! You can't begin early enough these days." It was Appa's turn to appear suitably ashamed.

"You gave him a free rein, and now he's gone soft."

The words stung. Sub-60s, though, don't get to retort. And for the over-90s, there's nothing to retort to.

"Tuition it is, boy," Thatha said, crossing me. "Find him someone good," he commanded Appa. "And make sure he begins right away."

We said nothing, meek in our acceptance of his diktats.

"I'd suggest advanced classes, but," Thatha shook his head, "you can focus on the board exams for now. I'll put you somewhere advanced once they're done. Even if I have to pay for it myself!" With this, glowering at the two of us, he left.

I looked at Appa, who looked away. If I expected succour, I'd have to seek it elsewhere.

***

"Tuition," I said later that evening.

"Hmmm." Tarun fell in that unique category of bus/carpool friends one has in school—placed in a different section from me, but living in the same area as us. He took a thoughtful puff and stared down a passing aunty who threw us a dirty look.

It was Tarun's idea to take our illicit cigarettes to a near-deserted park in a neighbouring colony. I thought it was pure genius. So far, though it was evident that the residents thought us ruffians, nobody had actually come close enough to question us.

"It won't be that bad," he said after a while. "All of us go." Tarun went only to please his mother. Tuition subjects—STEM—had always come easily to him, and always would. And he knew it. "If it helps, it helps. Join me at Rao's, the momo-wallah outside is killer."

"I don't think group classes are on the table. I have a feeling they're going to catch hold of some personal terror. As if Rekha isn't bad enough."

"She knows, man, she *knows*," Tarun said, eyes glazing over. He made little bones about lusting after our maths teacher. The rest of us grudgingly accepted that she was better looking than most, but her advanced years, coupled with a strong dislike, if not loathing, for the subject, made Tarun's naked infatuation utterly revolting.

"Snap out of it," I said, blowing smoke at his face. He blinked.

"It's not like that. She *knows*, man. She just has—a communication problem." He looked rather pleased with this diagnosis.

"Yeah, well, she's certainly not *communicating* anything to me."

Tarun waved at an old man who seemed to have thought of slowing down as he trudged past. He glared, but hurried on.

"It's these fucking alphabets, man." I stomped on the stub with more force than necessary. "Came out of nowhere, and now they're edging out the numbers, day by day." For once, Tarun did not wax lyrical about the nuanced beauty of calculus.

The park had grown dark. A security guard pottered around, switching on some lamps.

"Chal, let's check out the new momo-wallah in the market. Bet he trumps the one at Rao's."

"In your dreams."

***

"There you are," Appa said the next day as I shut the door behind me.

I flopped onto the sofa, perspiring from the rigour of the evening game of cricket. Appa came and sat beside me, still in his office clothes. It was a conversation neither of us particularly wanted to have. If only I were Shankar. Fucker.

"I've been asking around," he began, feigning enthusiasm. "And I've shortlisted two tutors." My hunch had been spot on. Group classes? Only for those with 70 and above. Mid-50s needed sequestered attention, lest their idiocy afflict brighter kids with stellar prospects. "I think they both sound all right, but I'll let you choose." He paused, but I said nothing.

"Well, there's a chap called Ghosh. Retired Delhi University professor. Brilliant fellow. Runs classes near the temple lane, and students flock to him. Sixteen of them got one hundred per cent last year."

I sat up. The man sounded all right.

"He'd, uh—" Appa cleared his throat. "I, uh, took the liberty of having a word with him. He's agreeable to taking you on, but he'd like to take a small test before, he said."

I pursed my lips. The first tuition teacher I'd ever heard of, and there were conditions of calibre and ability even before I had a foot in the door.

"And the other one?"

"Ah, yes," Appa said, looking relieved at my decision to participate in the discussion.

"This fellow called Subramaniam. Aparna Aunty told me about him; he teaches at her school. He says he's ready to begin at any time."

I waited, but that seemed to be the end of Subramaniam's introduction. Appa rose and began making tea. I followed him into the kitchen, pondering my choices. I pictured Ghosh, the crafty Bengali, with thick glasses, silver hair, and a hooked nose. Minting money off students who were already smart, milking the anxiety of their unsuspecting parents. Probably kept a cane for the dunces who threatened his results, reputation and revenue.

And then there was Subramaniam. A friendlier sort. And well, Aparna Aunty was the vice principal at St. Anthony's, which always ranked among the top ten in the city. Maybe he wouldn't be as sharp as Ghosh, but he should get the job done.

"I think I'll give Subramaniam a go."

"Are you sure? This Ghosh—"

"Yes, I've heard that he's good out of the couple of boys who come to play. Fast bowlers from Anthony's," I said quickly.

"Well, all right," Appa said. I turned towards my room.

"Sidhu, wait." Appa took his time bringing his tea to the table, motioning for me to sit.

"Look, your grandfather, I, we all want the best for you." I could think of nothing to say, this conversation being the first of its kind for me. "That's not to say that you haven't always done your best," he added in a rush.

"I have! But all of a sudden, all that seems to be forgotten." To my horror, I felt a lump beginning to form in my throat.

"Yes, yes, we understand. And that is the very reason Thatha has very high expectations from you. Nothing but the best for Sidhu, he can't stop telling everyone at the *kovil*. He'd—we'd—love to see you do well, that's all."

I looked away. For someone who didn't study beyond the fifth standard, my grandfather had iron-clad views on education and the path it must take. By the time I was ten, countless men, young and old, had dropped in at our house, stopped us in the street even, gushing about the profound impact Thatha had had on their lives.

He'd funded someone's education, bought textbooks for another, and had even found a wife for a third. Each of them had but one message for me, delivered unfailingly with a patronising hand resting on my young shoulder. *Saravanan Uncle is a remarkable man. Do as he says, and you will ever prosper.*

Matters of the heart aside, *do as he says* comprised a simple formula: get yourself an engineering degree from IIT-B, D or M (even medicine was deemed an ignoble choice), a brief interlude of deskwork, austere living, and high savings. Then make your way to IIM-A, B or C. Then big bucks deskwork, austere living, and high savings, for the rest of your life.

Appa sipped his tea, watching me out of the corner of his eye.

"Well, obviously, I *want* to do well. Don't know why I'm finding the subject so tough all of a sudden."

"Yes, we know that. It's good of you to go along with his decision, even if you don't need it. But if it helps you get back on track, nothing like it."

Back on track. A sudden, alarming visual flashed before my eyes—of a large, unwieldy steam engine with my face plastered at its head, wheezing to a stop in the middle of nowhere. Appa rose, perhaps cutting off my words before I had the chance to form them.

"I'll speak to Subramaniam, then. You can begin tomorrow. Let me also go over to Thatha's to tell him." He hurried off, eager to share his report, leaving me alone at the table.

***

"I didn't ask for this, you know. Any of this." There are many laughing pictures of her, but when I need to speak, I always choose one that the others miss out—a straight, piercing look, a hint of good humour on her lips, eyebrows raised a fraction, as if the camera had caught her off guard.

"I just went along with everything. I didn't ask to be the only grandchild, or for that scholarship, or all of those exam marks. It all just…happened." My voice, tinged with defiance just a while ago, sounded thin and small.

She stared at me, polite, unjudging, and unquestioning.

"And now." I faltered. "Now I'm flailing. We're at the business end, and everything is suddenly in disarray."

Even as a small, sensible part of me militated against it—after all, it was just one exam out of many, surely Subramaniam would help me—a cry escaped my throat, bringing together everything I had worked hard to sidestep since my exam result. Pricks of shame formed in my eyes, and I let them flow down my cheeks.

Unwittingly, somewhere along the way, I had developed the expectation of sailing through unhindered, unimpeded by the challenges that seemed to vex those I had come to see as lesser-gifted contemporaries.

"And why NOW?" The tears gave way to their more yielding cousin. Hot anger bubbled up to my lips. "Why have I been led on to this moment? If I was bound to stumble, if I was destined for less, why not years ago?"

I stared at her, my chest heaving. A creak from the next room told me that Appa was up. Or perhaps I'd woken him. I imagined him sitting up, fumbling for his spectacles and pausing, debating whether to come over and pick up our earlier conversation. I lay down, clutching the photograph to my chest, eyes clasped shut.

Another creak, a groan escaping the bed as weight settled on it. I sighed, relieved, sure that he was doing the same, grateful for the silence from my room. Poor, gentle, well-meaning Appa. He really knew so little about these matters. This had been her domain. And she knew how to keep Thatha out of it, too. If he tried to bully her too much, push too hard, she had this way of drawing herself up to her full height, pursing her lips and saying, *He'll be just fine. I know what I'm doing.*

But *I* don't know, Amma. I no longer seem to know. Clutching the photo close, I fell into a fitful sleep.

II

"Hello? Hello, Sidhu?"

The line was crackly, disturbed.

"Yes, Appa, I can hear you. Everything all right?" I jammed the receiver into my ear.

"Hello. Yes, Subramaniam just called. He's broken his leg, can't walk."

"Okay."

"So—" Appa sounded a touch impatient.

"So, he can't come home?" I asked.

"Yes, yes, but you can go to his place. Take down the address quickly, I'm in a rush."

I took it down and hung up. I'd been only too happy to think that my first-ever tutor had gone AWOL without so much as an introduction. Though his place was not too far from home, having to walk it day in and day out, presumably for the next few weeks, seemed an added irritant, making the first hiccup of my life even more bothersome. *An inauspicious beginning,* I thought, as I gathered my books and made my way out.

***

My family consults two doctors—the preferred lives in a palatial mansion in Press Enclave, ex-AIIMS, booming laugh of the wealthy, gold teeth and all. But when the ailment is minor or the time insufficient, we visit the other, a stout octogenarian with white hair and a sharp tongue who sits in a cramped clinic behind the local market and treats his patients—mostly poor labourers from the slums that dot the underbelly of the market—at a nominal charge. It was in this congested locale that Subramaniam Sir lived. Appa had marked Dr Trivedi's clinic as a landmark, saying that I'd find the house in the next lane.

I wrinkled my nose at the gobs of dung splattered around the path. There was a reason that Amma had disapproved of Appa's occasional visits to Trivedi, cost-savings notwithstanding, berating him mercilessly for not making the trip to the glamorous Dr Khurana. I sidestepped a serene cow holding up traffic, avoided a cart piled high with vegetables and stepped into the lane beside the clinic.

St Anthony's was evidently a tight-fisted paymaster. Aparna Aunty seemed to get by just fine, though, I thought, recalling her diamond choker from the last wedding reception we'd all been to. Grinning at my own pettiness, I counted the houses down. J-161. This was it. Taking a breath, reminding myself of the necessity of my visit, I rang the bell.

"*Vaa,* come in," a weak voice called out.

I pushed open the unlocked door and stepped in. Incense and the clean, white scent of *vibhooti* assailed my nostrils. Even before I'd set eyes on my new guru, I was confronted by a full-length cabinet of devotion. Gods, young and old, male and female, peered down at me, flashing gentle smiles through knowing eyes.

I repressed a sudden urge to prostrate myself and beg for deliverance from this mortifying predicament. Tearing my eyes away from a particularly arresting Ganesha, I turned to my left to face my tutor. A balding, rotund man with a thick moustache and a plaster on his left leg grinned up at me from a cot that was reminiscent of a Bollywood jail cell.

"Devout boy, eh? Expected no less. I know your Thatha. Excellent man, Saravanan Saar." I bobbed my head in acknowledgement of this new, unsurprising factoid and looked around for a place to sit. The room ended before it began, the cot and the temple cabinet seeming to swallow it up.

Subramaniam Sir was old enough to have grown children, yet his house was devoid of any sign of matrimony. I couldn't help but think that no self-respecting woman would choose to live in such quarters, in such a state.

"Sit, sit," he said, shifting his legs with a grimace. Ever dutiful, I took my place on the cot at my guru's feet. Thatha would be proud. "Siddharth, isn't it?"

"Sidhu, Sir."

"I am Subramaniam Saar."

"Yes, Saar." It suited him.

"You've brought the books? Notebook?"

"Yes, Saar. Both NCERT and RS Agarwal."

"Oh, no need for RS," he said with a cherubic smile. "NCERT will be sufficient."

I nodded slowly with a silent apology to the renowned author and mathematician, dropping the decidedly more confounding of the two textbooks into my bag.

Saar hummed to himself as I flipped through the pages of the thinner book, unsure of where to begin. It seemed like we were equal parts in charge.

"Er, so," I ventured, my thumb pausing at linear equations, a topic I was not too allergic to. "Shall we begin with linear equations?"

He looked at me with mild surprise. "Yes, sure, though I was thinking APs."

"Ok, Saar."

"Could you fetch me some water first, though?"

I looked around and made for the tiny fridge in the corner.

"No, no, that pot over there." He gestured to an earthen pot propped up on a steel frame. Making my way across the Spartan room in two strides, I grabbed a steel tumbler kept atop the plate that sealed the pot and fished the water out with a ladle, feeling very much like one of those poorly drawn characters illustrating a chapter about Indian village life in a hurriedly commissioned social studies textbook.

"Thank you," Subramaniam Saar said, arm outstretched to receive the tumbler. As he gulped down the water, I wondered if he had been languishing on the cot, contemplating his gods and willing me to show up on time and slake his lingering thirst. I hoped he had a cook.

"Thank you," he repeated, propping himself up. "Now for those APs." We proceeded to navigate the murky world of arithmetic progressions for an hour.

***

"Late," Tarun said.

"Yeah, class stretched on for a bit." I snatched the half-smoked cigarette from his hand and took a puff.

"Tuition and all. Welcome to the dark side." Tarun spread his hands. "So, how was it?"

"Not bad." It had barely been an hour since I'd left the depressing little, sparse flat, but I recollected nothing. My only lingering memories from the session were the grinning Ganesha and the pot that yielded surprisingly cool water.

"Great," said Tarun with a sharp clap that startled a nearby toddler, who looked at us, wide-eyed. Don't worry, boy, years yet before you have to contend with maths tuition and tutors. "You're all set, then." Tarun stole the last drag, an infuriating habit.

All set. The toddler broke eye contact and ran off to his mother. Much like APs had fled my mind.

"When's the next maths test, yaar?" I asked, forcing a casual tone.

"Week after next. Just APs, I think. Easy as fuck. Chal, momo time."

***

"I spoke to Subramaniam!" Appa said, reaching for the rasam. I glowered at him. "Just to find out if everything went all right," he said, avoiding my eye.

"Why don't you just send Thatha with me to the next class?"

Appa chewed in silence. I picked at my rice. It was an uncharitable quip. Yet, I couldn't shake off the feeling that the purpose of the call had been to investigate not just the fact of my having turned up, but also my enthusiasm. And aptitude.

"He's taken a great liking to you. Said you were respectful, disciplined and smart. Sure that you'll come through with flying colours," Appa spoke with a dint of pride. I felt ashamed of my earlier jibe. "It was good of you to be sporting and go to his place. Hope you enjoyed the class."

"Yes, it was, er, fine."

"And you know, if your results pick up and he clears the essential concepts," Appa continued, rising, "we can always discontinue." He flashed me a conspiratorial smile.

The mere thought of life reverting to its earlier avatar was enough to perk me up. I smiled back and began to clear the table. Appa shuffled off to Thatha's.

***

"58.5?"

Every last insidious thought, dodged with the dexterity of a champion fencer over the last few weeks, inundated my brain. It was the second instance in a row that I'd barely scraped through, my marks in the latest December exams following a string of poor test scores. With each passing session with the gentle, slightly eccentric Subramaniam Saar, the ignoble reasons for my choice of tutor fought to surface.

Any optimism Appa and I had shared about doing away with tuition altogether had evaporated at an alarming rate. Subramaniam Saar had turned out to be everything that my cunning brain had desired—genial, unassuming, unambitious. He was content to work out sums with me as a friend might, gentle in his correction of my errors; never pushing, never harassing.

If I had earlier felt that my numerical acumen had slipped away in stealth, without warning, I could now tell that I was content to watch, a passive spectator alongside the mild Subramaniam Saar, as it trotted further and further away with loud, resounding steps.

If he expected that I would be hard at work in between our classes, practising away the hours, Subramaniam Saar never said so. And, as I watched Appa pace the room, it was well apparent to all that I never did so.

"How could it happen again?" Déjà vu, that most unnerving of sensations, hung thick in the air.

"I don't know," I mumbled, staring at my knuckles. *You do,* a nasty voice in my head spoke up. The student's regret, a viciously powerful emotion, caught me in its iron grip. Even as I struggled and flailed, it thrust upon me the happy memories of the past few weeks, carefree hours on either side of school and tuition—bowling my heart out, cigarettes with Tarun, kulfi and momos at the market, novel after novel picked up on the sly as both NCERT and RS gathered dust. *If only,* the voice jeered. *If only.*

"You've just not been working hard enough," Appa shouted. "You're doing this on purpose!" As with the last time, I had little to offer in my defence. "Thatha is not going to—"

"Not going to what?" Thatha walked in, smiling.

"Just ran into Shankar at the *kovil,* he came to give thanks for his results, it seems. Brilliant boy. Anyway, how did you do? Your Appa's been telling me you've been working hard, diligently going to Subramaniam's for tuition?"

Without a word, Appa passed along the green report card that was to be my identity until the next one came along. Thatha took a long, hard look. I sighed and braced myself. Appa turned away. I realised he must be doing the same. *Good of you to put everyone through this every now and then,* the voice called out.

"When is the board exam?" Thatha asked at last.

I looked at Appa. "March," he said, eyes on the ceiling.

"I see." Thatha handed the report card back to Appa. "I give up, boy," he said. "You're not cut out for it." I looked up.

"You're going the dunce's way, I see. Maths—nearly failed. Physics and chemistry—good, decent. Biology—or shall I say, rote learning—excellent! And English, social studies, French." He paused to shoot me a withering look. "Top marks!"

Tears stung my eyes.

"You're going her way," Thatha continued with contempt. "Threw away a glittering software career to teach history to the buffoons of the world. *Ably* supported, no doubt." He rested his eyes on Appa, who held his gaze, eyes narrowed.

"But even she, at least *she*," he jerked his head towards a photo of Amma on the wall, "*had it* in her to become an engineer first. *You*, on the other hand—"

"That's enough." Appa took a step towards Thatha. "Enough."

Thatha looked at us in quick succession. "All right. I'd ask you to look into his tuition, but you're not really in charge, are you?"

I wished I had something to say, anything, in my aid or in Appa's. My tongue seemed glued to the roof of my mouth. Staccato gasps of air were all I could manage.

"You just don't have it in you, boy. Cook up what you want, both of you."

He left the door open. There was a finality to his steps, his rubber chappals seeming to bid a firm goodbye as they slapped jarringly on the small slab of concrete that separated our houses. Appa moved across the room and shut the door. He looked pained, but something in his manner told me that this was a different pain, larger than me and my pithy report card.

"I'll be having a word with Subramaniam later," he said, tone curt as he went into his room. I nodded at no one in response.

III

The new voice was here to stay. There have always been voices. They pipe up when you summon, berate and soothe by turn, and recede when you banish them. But not this one, not this time. It had come of its own accord. And it made no bones about its purpose.

Why weep now? You made this happen. You knew it would. Why regret now? You chose this. You're not cut out for it. You don't have it in you. You wouldn't even if you tried. You don't have it? What's the 'it'? Think, Sidhu, think. Search that memory that you pride yourself on, and you'll know.

The tears stopped. I didn't have to search.

I have an enduring memory, albeit of a small incident by any measure. I was returning from a school trip—no, a day-long picnic in the winter. Fifth standard. It was dusk by the time the bus brought us back to school. A sea of anxious parents had gathered at the gates to fetch their wards. Amma was to pick me up.

I stuck my face out of the window as the bus pulled up, looking for her in the crowd. She wasn't there. I couldn't spot her when I alighted. I stood at the corner with the toothless gatekeeper as my classmates bid me goodbye one by one. Some gave me questioning looks. All had cars or taxis waiting, which sped away.

In a matter of minutes, the crowd thinned. Still no sign of Amma. The teacher-chaperone's smile turned plastic as she looked around pointedly, impatient to get into her own car and leave. Sensing my discomfort as the minutes passed, the gatekeeper bought me an orange ice lolly. Amma reached just as I was licking away the last drops.

I watched her fight with the auto-wallah she'd come with, implore him to stay back, drop her home with her child, and then shout after him when he refused and drove away. She ran up, sweaty and lugging along a bag of exam papers, gathered me up in her arms, apologised to the teacher, who wasted no time in escaping, took my hand, and walked me out of the gate.

I half-listened to her chatter about her long day at the university and the injustice of that accursed auto-wallah. We crossed the busy road, my small hands unable to help her as she lugged the bag along. Once we reached the other side, she set the bag down, and then we waited. And waited. Rickshaw after rickshaw turned us down.

My stomach rumbled. She joked about auto-wallahs being allergic to our side of town. I smiled a smile that did not reach my eyes. Half an hour turned into an hour, and still, we waited. Pressure began to form in my bladder, and I squirmed. Thanked my stars that my friends and classmates were gone, and would not pass by us in this predicament.

As the fifth rickshaw turned us down, I began to fantasise about a sleek black car drawing up before us, a uniformed chauffeur hurrying out, apologising for his tardiness as he took Amma's bag and held the door for us. I could smell the plush leather of the seat, the musk of the car perfume.

And that is when I had decided. Without knowing anything, without understanding, watching Amma flap her arms about, I had decided that I wanted in. IIT. B / D / M. IIM. A / B / C. Deskwork. Big bucks. Not the austere living, but the big bucks. And then some.

That's the one, the voice said, roaring with mirth. *A foolish stripling of a boy, dreaming of chauffeured limousines while inhaling dust at a busy crossing. That's the 'it', Sidhu. That's the 'it' you're not cut out for.*

I sat up, blinking in the dark in shock.

And you never were. It was a moment of childish bravado, a pipe dream that was destined to shatter someday. Just a matter of chance that it didn't happen earlier.

With this, the voice vanished, its own master.

That night, once we finally got home, after dinner, Amma came to my room to ask about the picnic, a brown package in her hands. Perhaps it was a coincidence, or perhaps she'd sensed something in my monosyllabic responses on the ride back home after the seventh auto-wallah had taken pity on us.

"For you," she'd said, giving me a hug and pressing the package into my hands. "Might be a bit heavy to start off, but I think you'll be able to tackle it." And with a knowing smile, she'd swept out of my room.

I turned on the light and, rolling out of bed, rummaged underneath for the book, now faded and dog-eared. Romila Thapar's *Early India*. I lay down, clutching it to my chest, and stared at the ceiling fan.

***

I drifted through the days, unmoored by a heightened self-awareness that I could not share with anyone. Little changed over the next few weeks. Winter stretched on. Appa had a stern word with Subramaniam Saar, who, in turn, was stern with me for a couple of classes, but soon reverted to his benign self.

My maths and class teachers commented on my sliding performance at the ensuing PTM, reminding Appa courteously that the board exams were inching closer. He said we were working on it together. But at home, he let me be. Thatha stopped visiting us altogether.

***

"Why didn't you come today?" Tarun said, offering me the cigarette and a matchbox.

I shook my head. "Under the weather."

He shrugged and lit up. I was lying, though I'd said it to Appa with sufficient conviction in the morning to have him merely nod in response to my request to stay home. I'd spent the day mooning around, flicking through books and old photographs. I felt adrift as never before. The only anchors of my life—Appa and Thatha—had retreated into their shells in the background.

The voice, after descending on me with that startling revelation, had vanished. Yet, there was some part of me, some defiant bit of ego that soothed me, told me that even as I let go, things would somehow be all right in the end.

"Everything, er, ok otherwise?" Tarun offered me the cigarette again, and I declined.

"Yeah, why?" There was a definite edge to my voice. The last thing I needed was for maths to breach this last bastion of normalcy in my life.

"Nothing." He hesitated a moment. "Let me, er, know if you need any hel—if we can solve some papers together sometime."

"Cool."

"We'll have to switch colonies soon," Tarun said a few moments later, breaking the silence that I had let follow. We looked around as the evening smog descended on the park, at the few aunties and uncles who had almost become acquaintances. They had accepted us as they might the installation of a new bench or shrub.

"Chokes me up, almost," I said, prompted by this poignant thought.

"We'll head to Everest Apartments next week. I know a good park there." Tarun grinned. "Oh, by the way, we got the forms today."

I blinked. “Forms?”

“The stream forms. Forgot you were absent. To be submitted by Friday.”

I stared at him.

“Don’t look so shocked!” He laughed. “What did you expect—it’s Jan already.”

“Y-yeah, I guess.” I looked away.

“I’m caught between bio and computer science, man. Both sound ok. Oh—another thing, you can pick eco with science from this year—I’m assuming you’ll go for that?”

“Hmmm, sounds ok.”

“Thought so. Chal, forget momos today, tikkis to beat the chill?”

“Nahin yaar, you carry on today. Think I’ll just head home.”

***

Subramaniam Saar’s leg had long since healed, but there was a tacit agreement between us to continue our arrangement as to venue. The exchange with Tarun from the previous day lingered in my thoughts as I stepped over a steaming pile of dung and entered his lane.

“No, what do you mean, all of a sudden?” Saar’s high voice, with a tone of distress I had not imagined possible, made me pause at the door.

“But—but—all right, Ma’am, but it’s mid-January! An abrupt change at this time. What parents? No, Ma’am, my injury. But, you *must* reconsider! This won’t benefit anyone…the children... I—hello? Hello?”

I stared at the door. Whatever it was, I felt like we could both use a day off. But then again, I was already there. Before my indecision could proceed further, the door creaked open.

“Oh, Sidhu, it’s you. Come in, come in.”

“Good evening, Saar,” I said, not knowing how to ask after the despair on his face.

"Sit, sit," he said, moving to fetch us some water. When he returned, I was relieved to see the customary softness on his face. "We'd better get a move on, eh?" He said, sitting back on the cot. "Not much time left, in a few weeks, my job is done, only practice papers for you!"

I shuddered.

"Met your Thatha the other day," he continued, reaching for the NCERT. I looked up, wishing I could say the same.

"He was asking about your progress, saying your marks make him worry. But I told him not to bother. You'll come through." He winked, as though we nursed a shared secret. "With some focused effort, I am sure you'll return a first-class result." I pitied his childlike optimism. "Let's carry on with mensuration today."

I stole a glance at him out of the corner of my eye as I worked on the assigned sums. No humming, no twinkle in the eye. He was staring at his damp, crumbling ceiling, in deep contemplation. I wondered, feeling a stab of guilt, if I should say something. Another adult, and staying out of it, would have been a no-brainer. But here, with Subramaniam Saar, we seemed to be co-passengers on this journey, not wanderer and guide.

Catching my eye, he broke into a smile. "Focus, Sidhu, focus!"

"Right," I mumbled, looking down into my notebook.

"Decided on your stream?"

"I—uh—"

"Thinking of computer science, is it? Most of my students are. Good option, first class option."

"Er, maybe."

"Good, good. Good to see young people so clear on what they want."

I shifted my weight and scribbled some gibberish in my book.

"Saravanan Mama has very high hopes of you! Good, good," he repeated, the words beginning to grate on my ears. "I am sure you will do very well. These engineers are taking over the world. Don't want to end up like me, a mere maths tutor!" The touch of bitterness in his voice, yet another first, was unmistakable. He rose and made for the water-pot again.

"I won't." I shut my book with a snap. "I won't," I repeated. Subramaniam Saar looked around.

"You said something, Sidhu?"

"Yes. I won't do well. I can't."

"Hain?"

"I'm not cut out for it, Saar." I rose to my feet.

"Siddharth?" I must have looked crazed. *There it is!* The voice was back. But its tone was different.

"I think I want to take humanities, Saar."

The voice was like any other now. I had befriended it. Perhaps it had been rooting for me all along. My words seemed to have shocked us both into silence. I had a faint notion of the humour inherent in this little drama as it unfolded.

A fly on the wall would have seen me, a restless teenager, on my feet in this cramped little room, maths books firmly shut beside me, and a middle-aged, corpulent man, face betraying the shock of the unknown, frozen in the act of taking a sip of water.

The fly would have chortled at my plight and zoomed out the window. Having nowhere to go, I turned to my favourite Ganesha in Saar's divine cabinet. Even he seemed to be laughing at me.

"Sidhu?" Saar walked over. "Are you sure?" He laid a hand on my shoulder. I winced at the unexpected tenderness of the touch.

"Y-yes," I replied, and finally, a sob escaped my throat. I buried my face in my hands.

"Come, now," I heard him say, hand firmly on my shoulder. I allowed myself to be led to the cot and dropped down on it, my tears punctuated by hiccups. I was also faintly aware that I had hijacked what had clearly been Saar's personal crisis and substituted it with my own, and the shame of this realisation only made me cry harder.

"It's all right, Sidhu, it's all right," Subramaniam Saar said from time to time, patting my shoulder. After a few minutes, sensing that I was winding down, he stood. "Come," he said, shuffling to the door. Mopping my face, I looked around.

"Sorry, Saar," I mumbled.

"Just come, Sidhu, *vaa*," Saar repeated, with an authority that had been absent from his voice in all these months of instruction. I obeyed.

"We could both use a cup of tea. And a biscuit or two," he winked, the second time in the span of an hour. The thought brought a watery smile to my lips. "Come along."

***

I hurried home, suddenly aware of the lateness of the hour. The sweet, milky tea and cardamom-laced biscuits lingered on my tongue. Subramaniam Saar's kind, if slightly bewildered eyes, flashed in my mind's eye. His parting words rang in my ears. *You run along now. Do the right thing and tell the others. Don't worry about anyone. You'll be just fine, engineer or not. I am sure of it.*

The words, the memory of Amma, they stirred, and the rush of confidence—a near alien sensation—lent an urgency to my steps, threw off the lethargy of the past many days. I rushed into our colony, almost running, when I bumped into someone.

"Sorry," I said.

"Watch where you're going, Sidhu!"

"So sorry, Aparna Aunty," I said, pausing as she gathered her shopping bag.

"No idea why you people are always in such a hurry," she grumbled.

"Er, sorry again, I wasn't looking."

"Oh, now that you're here, I might as well; I suppose it's no less than my duty to let you know."

My house was less than a hundred paces away. I gritted my teeth and forced a smile as I waited.

"Your tutor." Aparna Aunty sniffed. "That Subramaniam. We—St Anthony's—have let him go."

"What?"

"Yes, shocking, isn't it?" Aparna Aunty was clearly enjoying herself. "He was simply not up to the mark. The students were returning below-average results. Just ten 90s in a class of 35! Unacceptable. The parents began to ask questions, and well, we can't have that, can we? In a board year that too."

I could see him sitting alone on that jail-cell cot in that austere room, pondering the evening meal. I felt a sudden stab of guilt for not having offered to pay for my tea.

"Other subjects, as usual, my students put up a stellar performance—"

"Excuse me," I said, stepping past before she could say more, leaving her open-mouthed and indignant in the middle of the path.

***

The house was still the same. For some odd reason, I had half-expected Thatha to have taken down pictures of our family altogether. My eyes rested on one of Thatha, Amma and me, a rosy-cheeked infant, laughter on all our faces.

"Well?" Thatha cut into my thoughts. We had interrupted his dinner. He'd crouched his fingers over a mound of rice, clearly expecting this to be a short discussion.

"I have to say something."

Appa, standing behind Thatha, looked at me, the cares of the day evident in his expression. *Sorry,* I said to him in my head.

"We need to pick our streams by day after. I have—I will be taking humanities."

I looked straight ahead, through the window over Thatha's shoulder, into the inky night. I heard a sigh, though I was not sure of its source.

Go on, the voice urged.

"To address the obvious, I haven't decided what to do later. Though yes," I stuck out my chin, "I might take a leaf out of Amma's book and aim for History at DU. St. Stephen's has the best course. I'll let you know when I've thought that out."

The silence became unbearable as it stretched on.

"Will that be all?" Thatha was staring right past us, his fingers balling up a mouthful of rice.

"Chalo Sidhu, let's go home," said Appa, moving over to me and placing his arm around my shoulder, the touch reminiscent of another not too long ago.

A clang behind us suggested that the old man was helping himself to more rice.

***

That same silence crossed the threshold with us into our house. Without a word, Appa went to his room to change. Giddy with the action of the evening, I washed my hands and set the table. Appa emerged and brought out our plates.

"You're sure?" He straightened up and looked me in the eye, catching me off guard.

"Yes. Yes, I am."

We sat down, but he said nothing, continuing to look at me as though he expected more.

"I suppose I decided partly by elimination."

The edges of Appa's mouth curved upwards.

"But yes, I'm sure. Not of everything to come later, but of this, yes."

There was definitely a smile. The gloom of the silence lifted as we began to eat, albeit without saying any more.

"I owe you an apology," he said at last, once we were done. "This thing, this choice of streams, everything, just crept up on us. It shouldn't have." He cleared his throat. "I ought to have spoken to you well in time. Thatha loves you, but it's difficult for him to change. And it never occurred to me that you may need to discuss all this."

"Trust me, Appa, I didn't know one way or the other until very recently."

We grinned at each other.

"Going Amma's way, then, haan?" He said, his eyes teasing.

"Maybe," I said, as we began clearing the table.

"Well, at least you're doing it at the right time," Appa said, setting his plate on the table and gathering me in a surprise hug. I shut my eyes and savoured the embrace, deciding to save the story of my enduring memory for another talk, another day.

IV

"Oh, Appa, one thing I forgot to mention yesterday." I'd caught him just as he was about to leave for work.

"What's that?"

"I need a new maths tutor," I said with a sheepish smile.

Appa chuckled. "I was wondering when you might say that. Another thing I should have taken control of some time ago. Fine. I'll take care of Subramaniam."

"No, I'll go over later today. But can you speak to Ghosh? I'll take his stupid test."

Appa smiled. "Sure. Full of surprises these days, aren't you?"

"I haven't changed, Appa. I still want to do well. So, I'll deal with Ghosh if I need to. Could you give me Subramaniam Saar's dues until today, though?"

***

"Humanities I took."

We waved in unison at the frowning uncle passing by. We'd made our way to the Everest Apartments park that, unbeknownst to its gentle residents, was to play host to us for a couple of months. This one seemed quite popular, unlike the last, but then, we'd become quite bold. Tarun looked around at the park with a critical eye, waiting for me to pass the cigarette.

"This'll do. A bit more sun would've been good. But it'll do." He caught my eye and we burst out laughing. "I heard you," he said after a while. "Your wayward existence has made for interesting viewing over the past few months. Heard some teachers bemoaning your name as one of the causes lost to the desolation of the humanities stream."

It was finally something I could afford to grin about, too.

"But good, man. I'm happy for you. But sad you don't get to see Rekha from next year."

I shook my head.

"I'm changing tutors, too. Let's see about those practice papers soon? I'll come over sometime?"

"Done, done," Tarun said. I resisted the urge to hug him out of the blue.

"Today, at least, then, momos? Chaat?"

"Tomorrow," I promised. "Need to take care of something right now."

***

With not a little trepidation, I retraced my steps down the path I was now well acquainted with. The currency notes rustled in my pocket. The crisp paper felt soiled, unclean. I'd set out thinking that I'd conjure up a speech by the time I reached, but I was near Trivedi's clinic, and still had nothing.

Some other tutor—particularly the kind that my friends tended to describe—and this would have been nothing more than a polite parting of ways, the closing of a transaction. But the sheer intimacy of our lessons, their tone and tenor, the close quarters in which I had seen him, and finally, the conversation I had overheard; the tears and tea from just yesterday.

I began to wish that I'd accepted Appa's offer to speak on my behalf. I turned into the lane and blinked. A van, angry headlights on, was blocking the way. A couple of sullen men wandered about, stacking up odd-sized boxes inside. Flattening myself against the wall, I edged my way towards Subramaniam Saar's house.

The door was wide open. One of the men brushed past and made his way inside, emerging with the idols and images I recognised only too well.

"Careful with those!" A voice rang out from inside.

"Saar?" I called out from the door. "Subramaniam Saar?"

"Oh—ah, yes, Sidhu! Come in, but be careful, things are a mess."

I stepped in. Shorn of his personal effects, I could now tell how small the living room actually was. He was seated on the cot, now bare of even the thin mattress that had borne our weight as we worked.

"This was here from before." He laughed, following my eyes.

I sat beside him, pity, shame and gratitude coursing through me by turn.

"So, how did everything go?"

"Er—yes. It was all right, they'll survive."

He grinned. "Well done!" One of the men came in to collect what seemed to be the last instalment of items.

"It was good of you to drop by," Saar ventured, prompting me to gather my wits.

"Saar! Where are you going?"

"Oh, well." He paused, giving me a searching look. I fought to keep my face impassive.

"Something…Something has come up," he said eventually, looking away. "In my village. I'm going back to take care of it."

"Sorry to hear that, Saar."

"Sorry that we have to cancel our classes at this stage. I meant to call your Appa."

"I understand, Saar. Here, your dues till today—" I fished out the money from my pocket and held it out, cursing myself when I noticed his raised eyebrow.

"Came to the market to do our monthly shopping. But no matter, I'll do it tomorrow," I said in a rush. He accepted the money. "But when will you be back, Saar?"

"Not sure, Sidhu. We'll see." He rose. Taking his cue, I crossed over to the door.

"I am sure your students will miss you. And so will I, Subramaniam Saar. Thank you."

"All the best, Sidhu," he said, smiling, looking at me with those kind, luminous eyes.

Stepping out, I flattened myself against the wall once more, crossed the van, exited the lane and made my way home.

***

Shifting in the uncomfortable seat, I watched the squat, dark, hook-nosed, bespectacled man. Everything in the room—the clear whiteboard, perfectly arranged markers and dusters, neat stacks of papers, and symmetric rows of chairs with desks appended to them—screamed of efficiency, order, and discipline.

Mr Ghosh tutted for the fifth time. I winced. Finally, he looked up and handed me the paper. 20.5 / 30, it said.

"Now, I won't ask what you were doing all this time," he began in a clipped, business-like manner. "Nor will I pretend that this is an acceptable pass mark to enrol in my classes. What I *will* say, though, is this. You've been allowed to be, or become, careless and haphazard. But I can see a reasonably quick brain and some potential. And that," he said, rising and turning to the whiteboard, "will do."

"Thank you, Sir."

"Not yet, boy. We have plenty to cover and not enough time. We start with linear equations. Page 132, please."

He clicked his tongue as I reached for the NCERT.

"RS Agarwal, my boy. Always, RS Agarwal."

I hid my smile as I reached for the dreaded textbook and turned to page 132.

Epilogue

"How are you, Kurup Uncle?"

"Eh?" The old man behind the counter, ancient as the books he peddled, looked around.

"Hello, Kurup Uncle," I bellowed.

"Oh, Sidhu, it's you. Back so soon?"

"Semester break, Uncle."

"Right, right. Well, how can I help you?"

"Need this bound, it's falling apart."

"Oh, you poor thing," he crooned to the book, drawing it close to his chest. "Eh? *Early India*?" He peered over at me.

"Everything all right?"

"I may be old, but my memory's not too bad. I'm certain that Saravanan bought a brand new copy of this just a few weeks back, saying it's for you."

"Oh, that." I thought of the gleaming book, smelling of new, safe in my hostel room. "Yes, he did. This is an older copy, a special one."

"Good, good. I'll take care of it. How is Saravanan?"

"Just fine, Kurup Uncle."

"Ran into him the other day at the *kovil*. Claims you'll be the best journalist in the country!" He smiled, writing out my receipt.

I chuckled.

"How much will that be, Uncle?"

"Three hundred. But Sidhu, tell me," he said, putting away the tattered book and handing me the receipt. "You didn't want to do engineering?"

"No, Uncle," I said, handing over the money. "I wasn't cut out for it."

A Commute

"Thank you," Ravi said, alighting from the cab. Yet another trip completed. He negotiated his way past autorickshaws crowding near the metro station gate, the drivers clamouring for passengers, yet rejecting many hopefuls with a casual flick of the neck.

Pausing near the gate, he witnessed a heated exchange between one such pair; the triumphant passenger finally took a seat, ignoring the driver's dark mumblings as they set off. Trying to remember when he'd last taken an auto, he recalled its typical interiors—bland black, or electric yellow.

For the passionate owner, perhaps some film stars plastered around your shoulders, serenading you with imaginary tunes as you make your way across the city. Cars were all the same, no matter how many gadgets the cab companies added to woo customers. They never added to the character of the vehicle.

The cab was too much about you, drivers often even querying what kind of music or which radio station you preferred. The auto held no such promise. Ravi reminisced about one of his first dates, part of which was spent in the classic auto, throbbing speakers behind them vibrating to the beats of the latest Haryanvi number and preventing any meaningful conversation. No number of entreaties about the music had worked. That's just how it was. He'd ordered a luxury sedan for his last date.

The steady swarm of morning commuters jostled past, some muttering under their breaths at his stationary figure. He himself was often one such mutterer, never understanding why people wouldn't simply proceed to the metro entrance (why would you choose this very spot to ponder the meaning of life?). Today, he hung back. He was early, very early, in fact—a rare occurrence, for it was equally rare for him to get home to a waking household.

Sensing a lingering presence, the hawkers began showing a keener interest in him, and for once, he in them. The Delhi metro station economy was thriving. He smiled and shook his head at a seller of smartphone accessories, a newspaper vendor and a sock-seller. A hiss of smoke assailed his senses as he passed by a busy breakfast stall tucked into a nook on the path.

Labourers and office-goers alike huddled around the *tava,* tucking into crisp *paranthas* and *sabzi*. The shopkeeper's young assistant chopped onions with nimble movements, the gas fumes apparently neutralising the onion fumes and allowing him to call out gaily to passers-by as he went about his work.

Unbidden, Ravi's mouth began to water. In that moment, he was quite unable to recall the taste of the equally crisp croissants and salami that had been served at the last client meeting. He'd walked the path to this gate nearly every day for four years, yet it was only after last night, after composing the letter, after congratulating himself for it, that he was able to romanticise these otherwise mundane and unappealing surroundings.

What would tomorrow be like? This was never a question he'd had to pose to himself. A euphoria borne from the glorious uncertainty of his future—a sheer novelty—spurred his steps along. The riverine flow of passengers swept him in near the gate. He barely noticed himself crossing security. His parents often nagged him about buying a car.

It would have been an airy decision, thought today, bought tomorrow. He'd, however, stuck to using public transport, not out of environmental empathy or even a grudging civic sense, but for sheer practicality. He appreciated the predictability of it. Green Park to Sikanderpur could only take so much time. Chance your arm, however, on Delhi NCR's clogged roads, and you were sure to burn your fingers.

He swiped his card at the turnstile without a second look, then caught himself. Perhaps life—daily living—would not completely turn on its head a few weeks from now. There was no saying, though, the extent to which some things—the daily casual taps of the phone to order multiple artisanal coffees, for instance—would assume significance. The thought sent a chill up his spine and brought pricks of sweat to his armpits.

Attention. Train with destination to Huda City Centre, having eight coaches, is going to leave from Platform No. 1. Thank you for your attention.

Ravi waited for the women's compartment to glide past and boarded the next one. It was to be a standing trip, as usual. The office-going folk greeted him as they did every day—a bored glance, a half-raised eyebrow. Some of his companions peered into his phone as he checked for new emails. None. He smiled.

Fate seemed to be conspiring in his favour, for actionable emails had a habit of popping up near Hauz Khas, which he firmly believed was the deepest underground the metro went. He'd gone through too many critical calls battling choppy mobile connectivity and the rattle and hum of the train.

Did he have enough? Did the numbers work? For the millionth time, he tapped away at his phone calculator, trying to find some error, some discrepancy. None. He'd spent nearly a year's worth of metro rides running them again and again—there was little chance of unearthing an anomaly at this, the most critical point.

The next station—Malviya Nagar—brought in the usual influx. The office-going folk shifted inwards to accommodate more of their own kind. Before long, two men stood out, their unwelcome stench of sweat and stale alcohol pervading the compartment. The office-going folk exchanged uneasy glances. Showing scant regard for metro etiquette, the two men sank to the floor near the doors.

Was I polite enough? Ravi fished out the letter from his bag and scanned its contents.

"It's always about money, the stinking thing," the older of the two men slurred. Ravi's brethren wrinkled their noses. They eyed the man with distaste as his head lolled about with the motion of the train. A few grease-lined curls, skin grimy like his shirt. Bloodshot eyes, a pencil moustache, and an angry welt on his forehead.

"If only I could find work for five days, I could pay them all back."

His companion nodded. The thinner of the two, with a more sober, sallow, tired look about him.

The life insurance premium—Ravi had forgotten to account for it. He frowned for the first time all morning. It changed his numbers, even if only by a thimbleful. The slightest lapse of control, and things could go awry.

"You, too," the man said, as an afterthought. "I haven't forgotten your money."

The companion kept silent.

"You don't believe me?"

"I believe you, but don't worry about it."

"Just five days," the man repeated.

The train stopped. The doors opened. The office-going folk waiting at the platform took one look at the men sprawled near the doors and stepped discreetly into the next compartment. Though a minor irritant, Ravi was almost thankful to the men for warding off more passengers. His thoughts tended to slow down with too many people clustered around him.

Should he check the numbers once more—had he made any other mistakes—any other line items he'd forgotten?

"I'm not scared of him, you know," the man said, sticking his chin out. "He's a son of a bitch." The office-going folk glared. "Always on about dues. Bastard. He owes me money, you know, owes me a tidy sum, but of course, he's forgotten. A big man now, isn't he?"

"We'll handle it," the companion said. "We'll see."

"It's getting incredibly difficult," the man slurred, shoulders slumped, running a wrinkled palm across his greasy scalp.

The phrase stirred in Ravi's memory. A phone conversation. Last week, with his parents. Yet another tirade against his job and its inexhaustible, ever-expanding demands. They had been steadfast as usual, asking him to tide over the tough phase, mildly encouraging in the manner that infuriated him when he was having a tantrum.

He was always ashamed later on, of course—after all, it was the prized job he himself had craved and pursued relentlessly—but in such a moment, with every ounce of the burden of manning yet another graveyard shift (not that he had the luxury of working shifts) bearing him down, he could never help himself.

Why do you blame us for wanting you to do well? Wishing that you have the life we never could?

It's getting incredibly difficult. Did you expect me to suffer like this for the rest of my life?

The train lifted itself out of its subterranean lair. Sunlight streamed into the compartment.

"Where are we?" The older man looked around through bleary eyes.

"Near Qutab Minar, I think. But can't be sure. Listen for the announcement."

This seemed to remind the older man of something. He shifted his weight between his haunches.

"I tell you," he said, rubbing the wound on his head. "I told you before, I don't even have enough for the fare."

The companion remained silent, satisfying himself by looking at the hazy sky outside. A station appeared. The slurring man made as if to rise. His companion tugged him down by his shirt.

"Not yet."

"Just as well, I nearly forgot the tool-bag."

"Still a couple of stations to go."

The man swore lavishly, summoning the words from the very core of his being, the way Ravi wished he could at many points during his workday.

"Who does he think he is? Summoning me like this. I just need five days, what's a few thousand rupees to him?"

What's a few thousand rupees to us? Arpan's grotesque laughter as he tossed currency notes across the bar top was an enduring memory, but the image that had stayed with Ravi from that evening was of the bartender down on all fours, MBA-instructed protocol forgotten, grabbing at every last one.

The thinner man looked around and seemed to realise that the office-going folk were now following their exchange. He lowered his head. Seeming to take his cue, the older man quietened down and contented himself with muttering under his breath.

Ravi watched his fellows curl their lips in collective disapproval as the man extracted an unmarked green packet from his pocket, tipped the greyish white granules of tobacco onto his palm, and began to knead them with a practised thumb. It was probably this man, Ravi could sense them thinking, who would later contribute his profile to one of those ghastly images of mouth cancer that appeared in the government's anti-tobacco skits.

Glancing at the men hunched over the floor, Ravi felt a flash of pity, then shame. He could not escape the realisation that his pity came from a place of such rarefied privilege that such a predicament had never been, and would likely never be, suffered. Nevertheless, he could not help feeling slightly defensive about the man who was, in all likelihood, his father's age.

He was sure that the office-going folk themselves made their way through more than a few packs a day, but felt that *that* was all very white-collar, very different. A green corner of the tobacco packet fell onto the floor. As if on cue, a pre-recorded female voice announced in her clipped, cool, and rather incongruous accent that eating and drinking were not allowed on the Delhi metro.

"That's not allowed on the metro, you know," the companion said, no doubt warming the cockles of the office-going folks' hearts. Nothing like a bit of civic sense among the downtrodden. Ignoring him, the older man tipped the powder into his mouth and dusted his palms off on his trousers. Specks of tobacco merged with the Brownian motion of the dust in the compartment.

"You really shouldn't do that," the companion repeated as the two men rose. As if offering a partial apology, the older man bent and retrieved the plastic corner, depositing it back into his pocket.

"I'm not scared of anyone but him," he said, straightening up with a groan. The companion showed no surprise at this volte-face. "You know that. Anyone else and I'd rough him up just right. I'm not scared of any bastard. If I get a hold of him, I swear it, I'll rip his entrails out," the man said, alternating between wringing his hands and balling them up into fists. The companion nodded, bending to pick up their tool bag.

"I can't even pay the fare, I tell you," the older man repeated, his jaws working furiously.

"I am with you. We'll manage. Why do you worry?"

Ravi saw the man next to him allow himself a quick smile. Ah, the camaraderie of the poor.

The train slowed once more. The drunk man tensed, shifting his weight from foot to foot. His companion placed a bracing arm on his shoulder. No sooner had the doors parted than he swept them out onto the platform. The two men trudged away, one supporting the other as he limped along.

As they turned towards the escalator, the companion paused and turned, directing an apologetic half-smile in the general direction of the compartment. Then he led his friend away and out of sight.

The doors slid shut. The office-going folk heaved a sigh of relief. The smell of stale alcohol lingered on in the compartment. The train trundled on, zipping past the next few stations. More office-going folk shuffled in, filling the space near the door that the two men had left behind.

The next station is Sikanderpur.

On another day, any day, his heartbeat would quicken as the steel-and-glass of his office complex came into view. Mental lists would be made. Muscles would tense. And the sweat of his palms would make his hands slide down the pole he held for support. Today was different. His fingers dampened the sheet of paper in his hand.

He checked his phone again. Nothing. A peaceful commute; a rare luxury. Fitting, in some ways, for today. He could get used to this. And he would, just a few weeks from now. After all, the numbers checked out. There was enough. He had saved enough. The numbers worked.

Sikanderpur station. Doors will open on the left. Please mind the gap.

Muscle memory, reacting to this announcement, brought him to the doors. The office-going folk crowded around. He wondered how the two men had made it out of the station with no money to pay the fare. A desperate jump over the turnstiles, perhaps, when nobody was looking. Or perhaps, some kind passenger had allowed them to stick to them as they crossed, the way urchin boys often did.

Maybe he had it all wrong. Maybe he should revel in the fact that he could afford to have no idea how much balance his MetroCard carried. Maybe he hadn't saved enough. Maybe the numbers didn't work. Maybe a glorious uncertainty was a fool's paradise, a romantic ideal invented by clueless young people without a future, searching for a legitimate explanation for their wayward lives. Maybe certainty was the virtue that held the world together.

Maybe.

The paralysis that came with that word, that had held him back each day of the past year, came rushing back.

Why did they constantly tell the office-going folk to mind the gap? They weren't a bunch of idiots. The doors parted. Ravi minded the gap. He let his resignation letter slip out of his hand and neatly into it.

Perhaps he would buy a car, after all.

Bathing Limited

If it hadn't been for my rather odd habit of leafing through the least important parts of the newspaper—from a real-world perspective, that is—I would never have seen it. I was doing my customary rounds—Page 3, the closing price of every listed share, *Education Times,* obituaries, matrimonial ads, even corrigenda (after all, some poor intern probably burnt the midnight oil putting them together)—when I saw it, tucked away in a corner.

My practiced eye dismissed it as an ad for bath fittings, probably some poor swadeshi type who couldn't afford to pay celebrities to practise their orgasm faces while caressing taps and toilet seats. What brought me back, a few moments later, was this tantaliser:

The tenderest touch since your mother.

Swadeshi or not, I was right about poor. A tiny 3x5cm box, red background, **Bathing Limited** inscribed at its centre in dull black capitals, the italicised by-line underneath. And a mobile number at the bottom. *Contact* was all it said.

I pulled the paper closer, searching for a stray word or detail that I might have missed the first time around. There was none. The lack of detail appeared to be a deliberate omission. I stared at the number and, on impulse, reached for my phone.

Really? A pained voice popped up.

Nodding at the unseen speaker, I redirected my hand to the paper and turned the page. For all I knew, the enterprising advertiser may well be a pervert or predator.

If it were so, crooned another voice, *why would it refer to a mother's tender touch?*

I flipped back quickly and saved the number.

***

If you think carefully, you'll know who I am. There's a me in your life. Look back on your journey, to its fringes, think of the most peripheral characters—I'll begin to take shape. The dull, reticent student who sat at the back and kept to themselves. Neither too bright (thus finding favour with the powers that be), nor a dunce (thereby memorable for their quips and antics).

That person in college about whom people seldom ask, but when they do, nobody quite seems to know what became of them. The straggler in the office whom you call upon for help from time to time, whom you thank in your sincerest tone to make up for constantly addressing as 'you'.

I am all of them. My name is Srinivas. You can think of me as Srini if you please.

***

Over the next few days, I toyed with the number, almost clicking dial on more than one occasion, pulling back at the last possible moment. The ad and the number seemed the only link to this mysterious company. My internet searches returned nothing of note. I felt a strange attraction to it, fed by the artificial conviction that Fate had decreed that I, and only I, be the one to chance upon it, hidden as it was amidst reams of important newsprint.

Every now and then, I flirted with the idea of letting someone in on it, but instantly grew jealous—what if they went ahead and called before I could decide whether I wanted to? Of course, there was also the distinct possibility of them thinking *me* a pervert, or laughing at me for noticing absurdities that were clearly meant to be disregarded.

In any case, my options were rather limited. Anil in IT, my office lunch companion of a couple of years, had come to be a friend, but the office was a natural barrier to the growth of the friendship beyond something as banal as debating the merits of aloo gobhi over matar paneer.

The handful of friends I had made in college were dispersed over the country; this was hardly an apt starter to a conversation that had lain dormant for a couple of years. How could I explain my strange fascination with that intriguing byline, those 10 digits that I had begun to spend hours poring over?

I broke out of my reverie and forced a smile as Neha, an ops executive from advertising, walked up, mirroring my expression with a plastic smile of her own. She looked stunning in an off-white blouse and a grey, knee-length skirt. Drab dressing for anyone but her. Her heels clicked to a stop at my desk.

"Hi, just needed some help with my reimbursement from last week."

For the few moments that she filled the air of my cubicle with her perfume, I forgot about the ad and the number. Oh, Neha, if only you knew my name. I would have felt better even if I had been spoken of with an appropriate moniker. But unfortunately, IT was a guy and accounts, a department.

"Should be processed by the end of the day," I said, all too soon.

"Thanks, er, thanks!" That terse smile firmly in place, she marched off, nose in the air.

I exhaled the strain of the brief exchange, my fingers clattering gibberish into my Google search bar. I would have been perfectly happy to let these intermittent chats add a glow to my day without uttering a syllable more than necessary. But last week, at the copy machine, I'd overheard her groaning to a couple of girlfriends about some fuck up for which she would have to speak to the 'creepy Mallu guy from accounts'.

And just like that, our fleeting and extraordinarily mundane conversations became torturous. Not being in a position to challenge her characterisation, and having run through the petty and exacting cycles of anger and righteous indignation too many times to bother with them again, my acceptance of her label was complete and unquestioning.

And my solution—or shall I say reaction?—has been to stiffen if and when she approaches, wear that customer-care smile for the entire duration of her visit, and to avoid eye contact at all costs. It is plain as day that I am probably compounding the problem rather than weaning her away from her suspicions—but it is what it is.

Oh, and I am not Malayali. I am from Andhra.

***

Neha, Ramya, Srishti, Sharanya. Even now, the mere recollection of their names summons each of them to mind with astonishing clarity. They swim in and out of focus before my eyes, each stunning in her distinct beauty, each representing a discrete phase of my life, and each out of reach even for the most innocent of conversations.

Sometimes, when Anil talks about his wife, I have to suppress the urge to probe him about the ecstasy of a woman's touch. Absurd thoughts race through my mind as I hear about the most mundane details of matrimonial life—does she lay a palm on yours while handing over your tea? Does she caress your cheek before you leave the house? Do you greet her with an embrace...?

A horn blared. I blinked. A few unthinking steps had led me onto the road amidst the unforgiving rush hour. The sedan slowed as it passed, and its lady driver rolled down the window to glare. Her attractive features only served to deepen my reflections. As it sometimes happens—and I am not certain that it does to companioned men like Anil—I stepped back, forgetting to cross the road, took a look around the junction and they were there, they were everywhere.

My own brethren slipped easily off the canvas, and all that remained were the exquisite creatures for whom I would perhaps never exist. The eyes began to betray—the woman on the Scooty, with the yellow-patterned *jhola*—Sharanya. The smart executive in the passing hatchback was Neha. Ramya, the dainty housewife perched on the motorcycle, bangles jingling as she slapped her partner's shoulder, mischief in her eyes. Srishti, the graduate student on the bus, staring out at the world with those luminous eyes. They were everywhere.

I felt a collective gaze on me, a lone man, unattractive to boot, standing at a busy crossing, neck craned to look around through unfocused eyes. The traffic constable manning the junction turned and took a few pointed steps in my direction. Jerking as though roused from sleep, a crimson flush creeping onto my face, I hastened across the road and scurried on home.

***

The newspaper cut-out served as my dining companion as it had for the past few days. Pinioned in place by the edge of my plate, it glanced up at me as I chewed, inviting me to look, to take a chance on it.

I set down my spoon with a sigh. I could not fight the feeling that things were coming together in some queer way. Again, I reminded myself of my self-serving theory that I was meant to see it, to ponder and agonise over it even now, almost a week later. Anyone would be curious, but a stronger man, a family man perhaps, or even a college student in love, would have had little trouble brushing it aside once the initial intrigue had evaporated.

Most would have been quick to dismiss the ad as one for immoral services that had escaped the censor's eye. This was not unheard of; naturally, even such establishments needed to conduct 'business development' and could engage someone clever to make the suggestion in plain sight using the fewest possible words. In fact, I was certain that if I showed it to anyone at all, such dismissal would be swift and backed by righteous conviction.

I stared at the ad, re-read its bizarre by-line for the thousandth time. I could not bring myself to believe that this was a peddler of happy endings. It could be accused of being mysterious, evasive, obscure—but somehow, in the tone of the few words of the ad, I was unable to detect sleaze. Again, I felt a throbbing pull emanate from the ten digits on the clipping.

I stood abruptly, leaving my meal half-eaten, grabbed my phone and dialled.

"Good evening. May I help you?" A soft, musical, female voice.

Cut it, cut the call, hang up now.

"I—er—is this Bathing Limited?"

"Yes, Sir, good evening! Did you want to make an appointment?"

"Uh, I—"

"May I offer my congratulations on being our very first customer, Sir! We're eager to serve you." Her voice gushed and bubbled across the line. "Sir?"

"Yes—the appointment. But first, I wanted to ask—"

"Lovely, well, I've already let slip that you'd be our very first, so we're wide open!" A merry laugh, rich and throaty, rang across. I let my question stick unasked in my throat. "The weekend is nearly here, and you sound like a busy man, so let's say Sunday morning, 11?"

"That, er, works fine."

"Perfect. Would you take down the address?"

"One moment." I fumbled for a pen and caught hold of the only piece of paper in sight.

"Yes?"

"No. 423, Green Park Market. Next to a shop called Evergreen Stores, and above a stationer's. Please take the stairs—sorry, but there's no lift—and come to the second floor." She rattled this off with the preparedness of a student before a long-awaited exam.

"Yes, thank you."

"May I ask, Mr—?"

"Srinivas. Rao."

"May I ask, Srinivas, how you chanced upon us?"

"The newspaper—"

"Ah, yes, the ad!" She laughed aloud. I shut my eyes in a bid to memorise the sound, to be able to recall it at my pleasure. It chimed in my mind's ear and slipped away, leaving playful strains behind. "I was worried nobody would notice. Well, thank you for calling, Srinivas! I look forward to seeing you on Sunday."

The line went dead. I breathed in deeply, savouring the memory of her voice, that laugh, the thrill of the immediacy with which she had presumed my schedule and proceeded to call me by my name. With a start, I realised that I'd forgotten to ask hers.

***

I struggled, over the next couple of days as I waited for the appointed hour, to recall each contour of the conversation, the quick dispatch of ceremony, the softness of voice giving way to gay sparkle, the tinkle of her laughter, the pleasing intimacy of a first name.

In the daze of the days, I pieced together my image of her. She couldn't be older than I. There was a distinct youth to her manner of speaking. She spoke flawless English—a convent education, perhaps. She began to form—petite, jet black flowing hair, laughing eyes, a regal nose, full lips. Slowly and steadily, she was taking shape, growing more vivid for me as we drew closer to the appointment. But if I gazed too hard, focused too much, she vanished.

***

On the morning of, I awoke, tired, jittery, and late. I had slept poorly. With distance and time firmly between me and this morning, it had been easy to reflect on the conversation and to fantasise about this moment. Now, as I rushed to get ready, my initial misgivings found me again.

It could turn out to be an elaborate honey trap, aimed at the lunatics who perused even the obituaries with interest. Yet, she had spoken with the eager confidence of the new grocer or florist around the corner. In sweet but clear tones, and in perfect English.

I caught my reflection in the mirror as I hurried to the door. A plain grey shirt, black trousers to match. Couldn't go wrong with that. I had forgotten to ask—or rather suppressed my desire to ask—for details of any kind whatsoever. How much, how long, dress code and so on. If she hadn't proposed the time and instructed me on the place, I might have forgotten to ask about those, too.

So, really going through with this, then?

Stroking my hair into place and shrugging at myself, I gathered my wallet and keys and locked the door behind me.

***

That the address was located in a crowded market was heartening. Dodging pedestrians and rickshaws, avoiding sundry hawkers and vendors and crossing rows of shops, I finally stepped before No. 423. It was an old building, blue at one time but grey now, desperately in need of a solid facelift. I spotted a passage leading to the staircase beside the shop on the ground floor. With a deep, gasping breath, I strode ahead and began making my way up the stairs.

Presently, I stood at the door to the second-floor apartment. A plain wooden door with a substandard polish job, but with a gleaming brass plate at its centre, emblazoned with the words **Bathing Limited**. Seeing no bell, I gave the door three sharp raps. It creaked open.

***

As the congested layout of the market suggested, the apartment was cramped. More suited to a bachelor's quarters than to any sort of commercial establishment. The drawing room was dimly lit. I could make out a small reception area of sorts, with two easy chairs and a small front desk beside them. No sooner had my eyes begun to adjust than a woman appeared from an inner room.

"Oh, Srinivas, it's you!" She beamed, no sign of a question on her face. "Forgive my absence when you entered. I was brewing some green tea."

"Hello."

"Nalini." She extended a hand and brushed a cool palm and slender fingers against mine. "Do sit. I'll bring the tea."

Her long, wavy black hair, worn loose, presented a pleasing contrast to her plain white summer dress. She had to be at least forty-five. Short and squat, of wheatish complexion. Rude pockmarks lined her face, and a mole had chosen to adorn the tip of her nose.

The elegance of her movements belied her plump figure. The gentle curves and lines of her skin, dotted with the hints of wrinkles, perfectly complemented those lively eyes, that throaty voice, and her laughing mouth. Together, they spoke of a graceful ageing.

I sank into one of the easy chairs and looked around, making out doors to two other rooms. Little effort had been made to fit out or customise the space. The apartment was still very much someone's house. Noticing the main door still ajar, I suppressed a mad urge to dash out, leave this dim little room and this corner of the city behind, and not stop until I reached the sanctuary of my flat. But I had to see her again. She had to speak to me again. I rose and shut the main door.

Returning to my seat, I noticed a few brochures titled 'Our Services' strewn across a glass-topped table wedged between the easy chairs. I reached for one.

"Oh, don't look at those!" Nalini set down a tray bearing two purple cups on the same table and gathered the papers.

"I'm still picking designs, see," she said, showing me the cover—only the cover—of each by turn.

"That one's nice," I offered, surprising myself, pointing at a mauve cover with pale black letters.

She grinned. "I think so too! Anyway, Srini—is it all right if I call you that?"

I nodded. She settled into the other easy chair and handed me a cup.

"You don't have to look at any brochure. I know just what you need." She shot me a disarming smile. Flustered, I stared into the grey-green liquid.

"I apologise for the cramped quarters." She sipped her tea. "We're looking out for a larger space, of course."

"When did you—er? How—?"

"Oh, of course!" She sat up, eyes shining. "Let me tell you a bit about us. Bathing Limited. A most fundamental service, isn't it?" A titter. "That's what we thought, one fine day, just a few weeks ago."

"We?" I looked around.

"Oh, there's nobody here," she said, with an airy wave of the hand. It was an odd way to address my question. I was torn between enjoying our solitude and wishing that the place had been larger, livelier, buzzing with activity.

"My co-founders are all operating solo dos. In other cities. We thought it'd catch on faster that way."

"Oh, I see."

"Four cities to begin with. Many more soon, we hope." The sincerity of her tone made me hope along with her.

Her enthusiasm matched that of a precocious twenty-something toying with business, raising the hackles of cigar-smoking, paan-masala munching boardroom gentlemen. Incongruous. Every word, every sentence she spoke begat questions. They tumbled through my mind, each jostling for space and primacy. But I could not bring any to my lips. Looking at her serene face as she sat there, cup in hand, legs folded underneath her, it seemed rude to clutter this peace with the burden of answers.

"Well, enough chit-chat, shall we get to work?" She set her cup down. I followed suit, though I'd barely taken a couple of sips.

"You'll find everything you need in that room." She pointed ahead of us to the door on the right. "Once you're done, you can join me in that one."

Not waiting for any acquiescence from me, she crossed over to her room and disappeared inside. Finding my feet a moment later, I walked to the anointed door.

***

Two full-length almirahs and a divan greeted me. The room seemed to open out into a veranda, but the closed door and drawn curtains kept the sunlight out. Easing out of my sandals, I stepped into the soft white slippers that lay by the door and seated myself on the divan. A bathrobe lay on it, and within its neat folds, a plastic packet.

Easing it open, I stared at its contents. Nothing but some translucent white fluff. Clutching it between thumb and forefinger, I extricated from the packet what could only be some kind of see-through underpants.

"Ready when you are!" Nalini called from the next room.

"Y-yes."

I undressed slowly. As if in answer to my searching eyes, I spotted a couple of hooks nailed onto the back of the door and hung my clothes up. Feeling goosebumps on my naked skin, I toyed with the underpants, turning them over to figure out the right way up. Shrugging at no one, I pulled them on, immediately conscious of how exposed I was.

Wishing that the fabric had been thicker, I slipped on the robe, grateful for its sanctuary. With a pang, I realised that I would be leaving behind some dear belongings—my wallet, watch and keys—unattended. But the time to doubt and distrust seemed well past. Throwing my hanging trousers a last look, I stepped through the door and pulled open the adjoining one.

"There you are," Nalini said. She'd pulled her hair back into a bun, accentuating the blemishes of her face. But her eyes looked softer, gentler, devoid of the playful twinkle I had already become accustomed to.

She rose from a small chair set before the door, revealing the room to me with a flourish. I gaped. Nalini giggled, turning the chair around to face the room.

"That's the intention."

I allowed her to lead and seat me on the chair. Unlike the others, this room had been torn apart limb from limb and transformed into a glittering bath chamber. To call it a bathroom would be a slight, this magnificent chamber that gleamed and hummed a mere foot away from its drab cousin next door.

It was bright, lit by two large lamps that rested on a shining white vanity counter directly across from where I sat. Everywhere I looked, marble or ceramic of complementary hues shone. Ambient piano notes floated by. Hand and body towels lay strewn around. A round bathtub of ivory marble occupied one length of the room.

At the opposite end stood a majestic shower cubicle, glistening invitingly in the subtle yellow light. Closing my eyes, I inhaled. My untrained senses could identify only lavender and jasmine from among the myriad scents swirling in the air. Nalini laid a hand on my shoulder. I caught her eye in the mirror.

"Ready?" She whispered, holding my gaze. I nodded.

Raising me by the shoulders, she reached around my waist and eased the robe off. I revelled in the warmth of the room. My exposed skin was a fact, but I felt a queer calm descend upon my body. Emboldened, I stepped towards the tub, eager to feel the cold caress of its stone.

"Not there," she said, taking my hand and leading me to the shower, picking up some unmarked bottles from the vanity on the way.

"I told you, I know just what you need."

Tingling, I stepped in. The cubicle was the largest I'd ever seen, accommodating both of us with room to spare. She set the bottles down on a ledge and turned to face me, eyes boring into mine. Abashed, I averted my gaze.

Reaching around me, she turned the water on. I winced, bracing myself for an initial stream of cold. But the flow that I felt pour down on my back was warm, perfect. I stepped back, shutting my eyes and letting it envelope me.

"I'd set the temperature in advance."

"Glorious," I managed.

There were no questions, nothing to suggest that she was at my beck and call, that I was to be fussed over and pleased. Yet, she seemed completely in control, aware of my every pore, taking her pleasure in mine. I sensed her step around me and turn the water off. Stray drops trickled off my neck and between my shoulder blades, making me shiver.

"Let's get to work, shall we?"

I opened my eyes and nodded. Taking a bottle off the ledge, she tipped its contents over my chest. The viscous liquid slid across me. She spread it evenly with artful, nimble fingers, never employing more than her fingertips.

"So, how was your week?"

"It was—"

A sigh escaped me as she used the spread of both her palms to rub the soap over, gathering lather with her firm, purposeful strokes.

"Usual," I mumbled.

"Usual? And what is that?"

"It was, uh, office is okay." Standing behind me, she was now working my shoulders and arms, scrubbing away. I groaned. My body was responding to her of its own accord, muscles relaxing, arms extending, acceding to her silent commands.

"And where do you work?" She turned on a single stream of water and stood back, patting the soap off in places.

"Azure Computing Solutions."

"Oh, engineer, then?"

"Accounts," I murmured. "The most boring department in the world."

"But the company would fall apart without you, Srini!" There was a hint of humour at the corners of her lips, but I did not feel mocked.

"It wouldn't, but thank you for saying that." I had a vague grasp, in some unwelcome corner of my mind, of the incredulity of it all, of standing near naked before a middle-aged woman in a bathroom, tucked away inside a shabby apartment overlooking a clamouring market, dripping wet, underpants gone from translucent to sheer, of having her send shivers down my body as she smoothed my hair, and of discussing my work with her in the midst of it all.

I shut my eyes and brushed the absurdity aside. Opening them, I brought Nalini back into focus. She was standing before me once more, the water off, a different bottle in her hands. The water had sprayed off me onto her dress, leaving it damp in parts, but she seemed unconcerned. She reached out and dragged a small wooden stool from the corner towards us and perched herself on it.

"Not married yet?" She grabbed hold of my right ankle and began to soap. I shuddered as her hands travelled up and down the length of my leg. The stirrings of arousal sprouted in my mind for the first time since that phone call three days ago, though my body remained limp, revelling in the innocent thrill of her touch. Freeing myself, I took a guilty step back. She looked up.

"It's okay." She drew the stool forward. "It's all right, Srini." I stared, beginning to relax again under her unwavering gaze. "Well?" She said after a few moments, taking hold of my left leg and carrying on.

"No, not yet." I laughed, a short, sharp sound that bounced off the glass walls of the cubicle.

"Only a matter of time," she said, reaching for the hand shower and running it across my legs. "And it'll be all right."

Perhaps it was the bizarre setting. Or the empathy with which she spoke, the tone of a mother gently chiding an errant child for dipping a premature hand into piping hot food. Or that I wanted to believe the words. Whatever the reason, feeling the cool water on my skin and her firm fingers rubbing the last dregs of soap away, in that moment, I believed her.

Some of my perennial melancholy, my unbridled angst against the world, lifted. She straightened, and I smiled, in pleasure, in relief, my body trembling in delight. As though fully aware of my mind, Nalini smiled a knowing smile back.

She placed the stool back in its corner and stepped out of the cubicle, returning presently with a plush blue towel. Ignoring my outstretched hands, she dried me with swift, efficient, matronly strokes. I closed my eyes once more and savoured the sensation, painfully aware that our session was drawing to a close. Before long, she led me outside to my bathrobe, draped over the chair I felt I had vacated hours ago.

"Moisturiser, comb, and a variety of creams and balms are by the sink. Towels all around. You can make your disposals," she grinned. I suddenly grew conscious of my bare, sodden midriff, "in this bin."

"Sure, thanks," I mumbled, eyes darting to the robe.

"Your clothes will be in the next room, where you left them. And I'll be out front." She stepped out noiselessly, leaving me alone in the ornate room.

The memories of the last hour—or was it more?—had already begun to snake their way out of my mind, carrying with them the details that I would fight to recall in the weeks to come. Sighing, I bent to peel off my sodden underpants.

***

She was waiting for me at the front desk, leaning over it and frowning into her phone. She'd changed into a loose black dress. I wondered if she was planning to step out after I was gone. The thought of running into her as she strolled down a sunlit street sent a pleasant rush down my spine. Would she greet me as she had today?

"Hello."

"Oh, hi." She looked up and grinned, as if seeing me for the first time.

"Er, well. How much?"

"Ah, Srini, you were such a good first customer to have, I'm tempted to say it's on the house," she teased. I blushed. "But what to do, have to keep the fires burning!" She giggled.

I smiled back and pulled out my wallet. "Well?"

"After your first customer discount, it'll be 1200."

I was tempted to ask how much the discount was, but decided to let it remain a secret.

"Thank you," she said, accepting the money. Her fingers brushed against mine, and I realised with a crushing finality that it was truly over. Sounds from the market wafted up.

"Thank you, Nalini," I said, hoping my words reflected the gratitude I felt.

In a sudden, unexpected gesture, she brought her palms together in a wordless namaste. I swallowed my promise to be back soon and stepped out of the main door, descended the staircase, and was soon amidst the din of the outside world, blinking in the afternoon sun.

***

In the days that followed, even as daily life set in, I realised that I still knew very little about Bathing Limited. There were no leads online, and though I continued to scan the papers, no more ads. None of the Nalinis I found online matched mine. Several temptations washed over me in waves—to set up another appointment, to tell Anil about it, to call Nalini just to check in.

I resisted them all. Work kept me busy. Anil would think I was lying, or mad, or both. Though I did want to see her again, I wanted to wait out an appropriate gap. And so, I meandered on, hugging my secret to my chest.

***

A couple of months later, as I was sifting through some papers at my desk at home, the ad fluttered out. A surge of excitement coursed through me. It was time.

Revelling in the rush of memories that this brought on, I grabbed my phone and dialled, eager to hear her playful, teasing voice call my name. The operator's cool voice informed me that the line was busy. I had no idea how they'd gotten word out, but it seemed like business had picked up. I grinned through a pang of jealousy at the realisation that I was no longer her only customer, that I would have to share her touch, her voice, her unabashed teasing, her empathy.

I called again an hour later.

"Hello." A deep male voice broke through the mechanical ringing.

"Er—"

"Bhaskar here."

"Uh, Bathing Limited?"

"Sorry?"

"Uh, sorry, maybe I have the wrong number. Nalini?"

"No idea. I got this number just a couple of weeks ago."

"I—"

The line went dead. I checked the number, re-checked against the ad. No mistake.

***

The proprietor at Evergreen Stores gave me a look as I rushed past and bounded up the stairs. As I rounded the last flight of stairs onto the second floor, a stout padlock greeted me. The nameplate seemed to have been ripped off by force. I ran my fingers over the holes it had left behind. Memories of her compassionate touch, her staunch empathy, tugged at my heart.

The bath chamber—what had become of it? Closing my eyes, I imagined walking around it, led by her, to the tub this time. Had she been able to take it with her? Had she simply relocated to a larger space, as she had mentioned? Were they operating out of a different city?

Dazed, I made my way downstairs and shuffled across the road, barely registering the passing traffic. A teashop at the corner caught my eye and I paused, deciding to gather my wits over a steaming cup. If only she had left something, anything behind, any tiny detail, even her last name! I kicked myself for my incuriosity that day and cursed into my tea.

"Looking for something, Sir?"

I looked up. Mr Evergreen flashed paan-stained teeth at me.

"I—er, no, nothing."

"You weren't going to the second floor of 423 by any chance, were you?"

"So, what if I was?"

"Ah, Sir, great property, Sir, you are an astute businessman, I can tell."

He clearly had no memory of my previous visit. Google be damned. This balding, paan-spitting buffoon seemed to be my only hope.

"Er, that's right. I've heard Green Park market is an ideal location."

"Arre, Sir, you may be young, but you keep yourself well informed, eh?"

"But what's a prime property like this doing, lying vacant?" My heart began to race.

"Oh, you won't believe it, Sir, it was mortifying." He held the suspense, taking his time to stuff a fresh paan into his mouth.

"The previous tenant, *my* previous tenant, a lady, seemed nice and all, told me she wanted to open a small showroom for bath fittings. She had all the licenses, didn't she? But who knows what's real and what's fake in today's world."

"Then? Then what?"

"Ministry raided her, Sir. Spurious filings and all! There was a police jeep and everything. She was running some sort of," he leaned in and lowered his voice to a whisper, "sex racket, Sir!"

Realising his folly, his face contorted into a grimace. I shut my eyes tight, clinging to the memory of that satin caress, the soothing tone, the tinkling laughter that would haunt me forever.

"But the *property* is first rate, Sir! Hey, wait, Sir, where are you going?"

The Bet

The tents were noisy that night. A lone figure walked away from the screams and exclamations of joy or disgust, often accompanied by gratuitous unsolicited advice. A man less accustomed to tradition may have found it difficult to tear himself away, but as the appointed hour had drawn close, the Colonel had stood, excused himself, and marched out with resolute strides.

A young chap in a crumpled tracksuit, splashing water from the jug in his hand, hurried past without a greeting. The Colonel forgave him the misdemeanour. They were all human, of course, though trained to suppress every last ounce of human instinct.

The barbed wires, three neat rows seeming to hum in unison like sprinters locked in a race, soon came into view. The chill of the late February desert crept past his fatigues and into his bones. The Colonel shuddered and buttoned his jacket up to his chin. A scream of unbridled joy sounded in the distance behind him. He sighed in relief and checked his watch as he drew up to the chasm that separated him from his appointment. Five minutes to go.

"Fuck," he muttered, looking around. There was no seat in sight—not that there ever was at this spot, but on each of the previous three occasions, he had arranged for a seat well in advance. No, it simply wouldn't do to remain standing. Tugging at the salt-and-pepper of his moustache, he reached for his wireless with some reluctance.

"Chair *lao*. 10th milestone."

The response tarried. The Colonel began to tap his foot on the sandy earth.

"Ji *janaab,*" came the reply eventually.

The Colonel clicked his tongue. "*Jaldi.*"

He soon heard faint twin footsteps from the other side. The Colonel glanced at his watch once more. Not a moment early, nor a moment late. The Major was predictable to a fault. He soon sighted two upright figures, the taller one leading the other, walking towards him with brisk steps. No more than a hundred metres from where he stood.

The Colonel cursed and was about to growl into his wireless when he heard sprinting boots behind him. He turned. A young, panting *havildar*, a foldable chair clutched under his left arm, ran up and saluted. The Colonel knew him by face, but to his embarrassment, was unable to recall the young man's name.

"Thank you, er, *havildar*."

"*Maafi*, Colonel, I took some time, but there's pandemonium inside, and seats are at a premium—"

Breaking off, the *havildar* abruptly drew himself up to his full height and narrowed his eyes over the Colonel's right shoulder. The veins in the earnest young chap's neck bulged as he gnashed his teeth.

The Colonel swivelled around. The Major, not a hair out of place, stood no more than eight feet away, not quite at attention, feet slightly apart, but arms at his sides in a somewhat formal posture. The Colonel envied the younger man's height and hawkish good looks.

Himself, the Colonel was, as his wife often quipped to their friends, ruggedly handsome—more rugged, less handsome—and had always relied on the sharpness of his uniform and the taut elegance that it brought out in him, where his hooked nose, sunken eyes, and lately, his emerging belly, let him down.

The Major, on the other hand, with his square jaw, high cheekbones and sleek hair, had often appeared to the Colonel to be a movie star play-acting at a military role, part of some border potboiler that would make waves in both countries. The Major's own young sentry, hackles similarly raised at the seething *havildar*, stood behind him, holding a plastic chair.

The Major drank in the scene and caught the Colonel's eye. His lips twitched. Clearing his throat, he said, "Good evening, Colonel."

"Evening, Major."

The Major remained on his feet and gazed up at the sky, appearing to wait for something. The Colonel started. Of course.

"Ah, yes, *Havildar*." He gestured to his left, at the spot right opposite the Major. "*Yahan* chair *lagao*."

Breathing hard, the *havildar* tore his eyes away from his counterpart, who smirked, and got to work.

Presently, the Colonel stepped forward and took his seat. "That will be all, *havildar*. You may return to the festivities. And," he eyed the other two, "say a prayer on your way."

Grinding his teeth, the *havildar* curled his lip at the wires. A faint roar erupted in the distance. The wrong side. The Major's lackey grinned. Shooting the Colonel a fearful look, the *havildar* struck a rushed salute and galloped off.

Settling back in his chair, wishing he'd brought some refreshment along, the Colonel watched the same bit of theatre play out across the wires. The Major appeared to have given his chap a quiet dressing down, for he reverted to the generally terse and expressionless face expected of all of them as he busied himself.

"Radio over there. Colonel *ki taraf*," the Major said, once he was seated. "*Chalao*, volume *badhao*."

The ancient instrument—a birthday present from an ageing uncle, ex-army himself, the Major had explained at the same spot several years ago—crackled to life. An old Hindi song streamed through, delightfully unaware of its incongruity in the space it filled.

"That will be all. *Jao*."

Unable to resist, the bearded young man tilted his body ever so slightly towards the wires as he saluted the Major in an exaggerated fashion. The Colonel shook his head and smiled. The music continued as the young soldier marched off.

"Amidst all this, the question is," the Major began, a few moments later, leaning forward towards the radio, "who the bloody hell is listening to this trashy old grandfather music on this electric evening?"

The Colonel chuckled. The music disappeared in a burst of static.

"*And that's cleared the ropes*," the commentator's excited British accent burst through. "*India need 58 off 44, five wickets in hand.*"

The Major sighed, looked up and grinned.

"Fancy changing your wager, Iqbal Sa'ab?"

"Never," the Colonel said politely.

"I would if I were you."

"That's because you're an inexperienced fool."

The Major leaned back and laughed. "Suit yourself, I'm a bit short on cash this month anyway."

"*55 off 42. Don't go anywhere, folks, this one's going down to the wire.*"

***

"New recruit?" The Colonel asked, as the Major lifted a flask off the ground and unscrewed the lid.

The Major nodded. "Several of them, swarming all over the place. It's a circus on the best of days." He poured out a cup of steaming liquid into the lid of the flask, doubling it up as a cup. "I'd offer you some tea, of course, but—"

"—then you'd have to poison it."

Both men snickered.

"Just tea tonight, though?"

"If man has discovered a beverage that guarantees the drinker's team a victory, you must tell me about it, Colonel."

"And that's a fumble on the boundary, FOUR runs to Rahul Singh, now that's a swashbuckling southpaw if I ever saw one."

The Colonel inhaled sharply.

"Cheers to a good shot," the Major said, looking at him over the rim of his cup.

"Cheers to the ICC, you mean. Trust them to always pick some bloody British chap to commentate on *this* match. A blind man could walk straight into the irony of it. Swashbuckling southpaw indeed."

"It's not just *some* British chap," the Major said, horrified. "That's Ian Jones! The all-rounder of the 90s! Come to think of it, a bit of a swashbuckling southpaw himself—"

"And the ex-coach of your team. Yes, yes, I know. Still, when the English commentary at an Indo-Pak match is so lyrical, it almost makes you miss dear old Ramiz."

The Major choked and spluttered on his sip of tea. The Colonel strained to catch the commentary over his hysterics.

"Some of the shoulders drooping on the field, it's not looking so rosy for the Men in Green here."

"Ramiz!" The Major said once he'd recovered sufficiently, coughing through his laughter. "He'd say, 'and that's a fantastic shot by the youngster', all hang-dog sober, if the batter's name were Rahul. And pop a blood vessel waxing lyrical over the same shot by a batsman named Abdul. Or Junaid. Or Iqbal." The Major winked.

"I hear the PMs are watching," the Colonel offered in response.

"Really? What are they even doing there?"

"Some global summit. Not too fond of the papers, are you?"

"Must've missed it," said the Major, chastised. "Wonder what they talk about during the heat of the game, sitting amidst thousands of roaring fans."

"What I wonder," the Colonel said, leaning forward, "is whether our PMs are wagering men, too."

"That's a skier, it's swirling up in the air, a birdie if I ever saw one, and Zubair Ahmed is camping underneath it—"

Both men heard the breeze pick up and whistle into their ears, for none breathed.

"And 'e's gottem! He has got his man, Pakistan's best fielder is safe as a house, and he doesn't let that slip through those bucket hands."

The din of the stadium floating out of the radio matched the screams and cheers from their respective garrisons.

"Would *you* like to change your wager, Major? You seem a little pale there."

Saying nothing, the Major drained his cup and reached for his flask once more.

"It's down to 45 off 33 for India, with just four in hand. You can't, you just can't ask for a better World Cup semi-final than this. It's India, it's Pakistan, it's at the Mecca of cricket, it's better than the Mohalis and the Manchesters and the Jo'burgs of the past. It's all happening, it's all happening here."

The Colonel pursed his lips. "Still not a fan of the commentary, but I suppose he's got it right this time."

The Major grunted his agreement. "If I didn't know better, I'd say the F word, the way they make sure all these matches get so tight—"

"And that's bowled 'im! That's the end of KR Satish, no pinch-hitting from him today. Singh is getting stranded at the other end here, as the Pakistanis erupt. Could this be it, could this be the day, could this be the first—?"

The Colonel whistled. The Major's hand shook as he poured his second round of tea.

"It *is* a Friday, after all," the Colonel said, shooting him a sly grin. "Who knows, another day and Zubair might have dropped that catch."

"I thought you never believed that kind of thing."

"I don't, but today's as good a day as any to start. On that note, aren't we a bit decked up for the match?" The Colonel tapped the centre of his unibrow.

Flustered, the Major made as if to rub the vermillion of the *tikka* off his forehead, then thought better of it.

"Didn't think it was visible," he muttered, smoothing his hair back in irritation. "But no, this was routine, nothing related to cricket. As if the two are linked."

"Really? According to the papers, the entire subcontinent has been at prayer the whole of the last two days."

"Even the Bangladeshis?"

"Why not? I'm sure they feel they've got some historical bone to pick in this entire mess."

"Well, then, perhaps this Friday business has got something to do with the score, too. Though God knows it's not worked in the past."

"*You could slice the pressure with a knife on this ground. India were coasting, but against the run of play, it's now ten an over required with only three in hand, and their recognised batter not getting enough strike.*"

"Time out," the Major declared, reaching for the radio.

"Really, Major?" The Colonel said, as Hindi film music resumed and streamed through the gap between them.

"Ah, we always miss some of the match getting here and setting up. We'll just pretend that there was a—what do they say? Technical snag."

A yesteryear playback king crooned in his clean, happy, cherubic voice about the many wonders of his chosen lover. One of his wife's favourite songs, the Colonel realised. Letting go of the absurdity of the settings, he began to hum along.

"They're finally talking of getting me hitched," the Major blurted out, as if he had sensed the older man's mental shift.

"Finally?"

"Well, yes, I avoided the topic for a time. Which girl would want to share this life?" He waved a hand across the barbed wires, over the sandy spread of the black desert. "The threats, the uncertainty, the," the Major stopped and looked around, "politics of it."

The Colonel grunted.

"Being a community poster boy alone is tough enough. The questions, the media glare, the—" The Major paused again, lips drawn across his angular face in a straight line, as if sealed together of their own accord. "The almost selfish admiration foisted upon me, balanced by the mistrust, the *publicity* of it all on some days."

"It'll wear off, son. I," the Colonel bit his lip, but went on, "know a thing or two about mistrust." He paused. "Anyway, what's her name?"

The Major brightened up. "It wasn't easy to find a girl, I daresay it was easier for you. But they found one eventually. She's young and lovely and too good for me on my best of days. Ruhani," he added, as if registering the question just then.

"I wish you both well." The Colonel raised an imaginary glass and toasted the health and happiness of the young, unknown couple.

The Major touched his beret in response. The song faded to the pensive notes of a lone violin. With its end, the bittersweet mood of its making dissipated.

Cries of agony and shouts of joy shattered the silence that the two men had allowed to settle between them. The Colonel glanced at the radio. The Major sighed and reached for it once more.

"Before you switch it on and bring us to the inevitable," the Colonel began, making the Major pause. "I must ask you again, out of courtesy, whether you'd like to change your bet and emerge a winner for once. There's a first time for everything, and after long years—decades—we have a well-oiled machine in your neck of the woods, against a transitioning, confused side in mine. Surely you wouldn't rob poor Ruhani of a thousand rupees." He winked, and the Major, radio in hand, grinned. "I'm nearing retirement, young man. This shall be our last Cup together. Think before you answer."

The Major laid a hand on his heart and declared, poker-faced, "A bet once placed and a bullet once fired cannot be recalled."

More cheers and shrieks. Aiming not to work out which side had emitted which—and sure that the younger man was trying to do the same—the Colonel shut his eyes and began to tap his foot once more, hoping against hope that he would have to part with the crisp currency notes nestled inside his breast pocket.

"*Jaldi*," he said, as the tuning static continued.

"Patience, old man, patience."

A few crackles, then silence.

"Is it over already?" The Major wondered aloud.

"And it's all down to this, all down to this. Incredible scenes here at Lord's. Pakistan are a wicket away, India, just one big hit. And here's Nazir Khan with his loopy medium pace to bowl the last over. Has the captain miscalculated here? Nazir's all he's got left! Rahul Singh taking guard, what an innings from him, but can he get them over the line? You'd have to say, even with all the tension, at just a run-a-ball, it should be India."

"Misbah? Hello, Misbah, have you been reborn two decades later on the opposite side to have a crack at the match you lost in '07?"

The excited voice was coming from a height now, so the Colonel knew that the Major had abandoned all efforts at military dignity and was, as was his wont, hopping about on one foot.

"And that's a dot to begin with, a harmless dolly, but Rahul can't put it away, and refuses the single, rightly so, you'd have to say—"

"Why did they, fuck, just why do they always have to let it get this close? It's fixed, it's always all bloody fixed, they're going to let it slip away..."

"Another straight one, gentle pace, And that's up in the air!"

Mouth dry, heart pounding, the Colonel opened his eyes.

"FUCKKKK," the Major screamed, dancing away from the radio as if escaping a venomous snake.

"IT'S SWIRLING UP THERE, THAT BALL IS THE WORLD CUP ON THE LINE, HERSCHELLE GIBBS, ARE YOU WATCHING!

LONG ON IS DEEP BUT LOOKS LIKE IT'S GONNA CROSS HIM OR IS IT?"

The Colonel had a sudden vision of the commentator's phlegm-soaked microphone, and despite himself, began to chuckle.

"AND THAT'S A BLINDER, OH HE'S TAKEN A BLINDER, IT'S THAT MAN ZUBAIR AGAIN, IT'S ONE OF THOSE HOPPITY HOPS, CAUGHT IT, TOSSED IT UP, HOPPED OUT, HOPPED BACK IN, THE UMPIRES ARE HAVING A LOOK BUT THAT GRIN TELLS ALL, HE'S GOT HIS MAN!!"

The Major was, by now, more than twenty metres away, palms clasped to his ears. The Colonel, suddenly aware of the weight of every pore of his body, shook his head and allowed himself a sad smile. The first time was upon him, and a billion others, at last. If only the streak had lasted out his lifetime. He sighed and rose.

"You can come back now," he called out over the excitable commentary, waving the Major back towards his seat.

Shoulders slumped, the Major dragged his feet back and lowered his arms. As he neared his seat, bullets sounded on his side, drowning the radio out. Happy bullets, aimed up at the inky sky, not eastwards.

"No," the Major mouthed, staring at the Colonel. He turned and gazed in the direction of his garrison, where the sloganeering, bound to continue through the night and for some days to come, was starting up. He took a few dazed steps inland.

"Major Lal Chand!" The Colonel called out. "Aren't you forgetting something?"

Almost tripping over himself, the Major turned and jogged up to the barbed wire, reaching into his jacket. Grinning, he fished out a small paper packet secured with a pebble and some black string and, leaning back, tossed it across the border.

The Colonel caught it with one hand. "Control your boys, Major," he said, pocketing the package. "And congratulations. Snatch the Cup from the bloody Aussies, will you?"

Possibly for the last time, he accepted the younger man's wordless salute with a quick nod and watched him sprint away to join his victorious comrades. Then, turning on his heel, he began the march back to his tent, though not as smartly as a couple of hours earlier. The prick of the unfathomable loss, to be dissected and agonised over for years to come, slowed his steps.

"There's a first time for everything," he muttered as he reached the outskirts of the encampment, passing surly faces, some with tears streaming down their cheeks, others waving their fists at the fireworks that blazed in the foreign sky just a few strides away. "First, and last." He smiled to himself at this defiant, boyish declaration.

Once in his tent, the Colonel sat on his bed and undid the white package he'd brought along. A single currency note—forever useless to him—slipped out and floated onto the mattress. He yanked at his bedside drawer and placed the thousand-rupee note with its three elder brethren. 2019. 23. 27. And now, 2031.

"A most profitable wager," he boasted to the empty room. As if disapproving of his wry humour, the four Jinnahs eyed him sternly from within the drawer. Shaking his head, the Colonel grimaced and rose to join his disconsolate countrymen outside.

Bravado

The doors to the metro parted. Roshan stared up and down the platform, eyeing the few stragglers that shuffled in. The train was surprisingly empty. Perhaps word hadn't spread. Or perhaps the trains peopled by public-spirited, justice-loving citizens had hummed past earlier in the day. Feeling a stab of disappointment, he stepped in, a moment before the doors slid shut.

He contemplated the rows of empty seats—a rare luxury. Nervous energy, an unfamiliar sensation, kept him on his feet. No doubt he had expected company on this short commute, and was annoyed to be left alone with his thoughts. But he would step into company soon. He was truly on the way. His palms prickled. Feeling one with the train as it hurtled towards his destination, he allowed the significance of the moment to wash over him.

Roshan couldn't help but feel that this was one of the defining moments of his life. In the past, he had scorned such occasions as insignificant rabble-rousing, feckless anti-statism from an otherwise dormant populace. Earnest friends had often asked, *if not now, when?* He'd dismissed the question each time.

It was an unfair tactic, he reasoned, an oversimplification of the unfailingly complex issues at hand, each of which required threadbare discussion, discussion he never allowed himself to get entangled in. His arguments always kept up with his comrades' desire to rush off to central Delhi; he was a master of intellectual self-defence, of shifting the goalpost till his adversary was exhausted. They always capitulated after a few rounds, leaving him not a little pleased. He had come to look upon it as a triumph of his arguments, rather than his obduracy.

He had grown accustomed to watching streams of people—several of his friends often in tow—parade past and make headlines, only to see the issue soon peter out. He claimed to be a champion of democracy, yet he took the fizzling out of these protests as a vindication of his own views, of his conviction that one has to pick one's battles. He had finally picked his.

A friend had once remarked, half in jest, that had the youth of the 30s and 40s been cut from the same cloth as he, independence would have remained a distant dream. He had taken fierce exception; of course he would have risen to the occasion had the circumstances demanded. The friend knew better than to probe the meaning of 'had the circumstances demanded', and Roshan was secretly grateful, for he didn't know himself.

He said all the right things, he knew, thought all the right things, read all the right articles, but somehow, he had never been moved to act. Some argument, some qualifier, some excuse had always provided cover, protecting him from the discomfort of facing his true disposition—that of a coward.

Yes, ladies and gentlemen, he thought, looking around at his few co-commuters, *I have been a coward.* He was almost disappointed when nobody gave him a second glance. To answer his friend, he knew deep down, as everyone always does, that he would have made for the classic colonial stooge. A civil servant, perhaps. Even a lowly clerk. Safe, cushy, cosy. Unlikely to suffer the slightest bother, let alone harm. No more, no more.

The moment of epiphany came the other day. The Indian state had opened fire on peaceful protests in some insignificant mofussil town. Of course, few were aware of the existence of the town, fewer still of the reason for the protest; perhaps this very fact made it a significant event in the eyes of the public.

Roshan winced as he thought of the hapless martyrs—did they know their end was in sight when they gathered near the factory to seek its closure? The very thought was ludicrous, akin to the suggestion that he should expect to be greeted by a stream of bullets at the end of his air-conditioned journey. Roshan shuddered.

The incident had taken its usual course already, in less than a fortnight. Opposition denouncement, government evasion, screamed debates on news channels, each more unpalatable than the last. Each new week churned out a fresh news cycle, pushing the town back into obscurity, till everything eventually died down.

But the image was unforgettable. Roshan could see it now, clearly, against the glass panel of the compartment window—a young, moustachioed police officer, standing atop a jeep, dressed incongruously in a white collared t-shirt and track pants, black sunglasses shielding his eyes from the punishing May sun, muscular forearms aiming an assault rifle at the unsuspecting public. The photograph had not captured them—it did not need to.

Another station passed. Roshan had always described himself as pro-state—not really a secret, but he had admitted it in as many words to only his most trusted friends, some who agreed with him, and those who were magnanimous enough not to question him. And, as he had often argued in the past, mostly to himself—why was that such a bad thing?

The state was a large, unwieldy, lumbering being with many preoccupations; surely it was unfair to expect it to respond to each isolated incident swiftly and fittingly? Surely its merits ought to be tested over a period of time? Surely, he reasoned, when it came to picking action or inaction, an experiment of the audacity and scale of the Indian state deserved one's patience and faith.

But that image had snapped something inside him. Of course, he was not ready to cast his every opinion aside, one nebulous thought to the next and the next, it was too muddled, it made him restless, caused physical unease. That would take time, and many muttered self-discussions. No, his need for absolution was greater, more urgent.

Why was the train not filling up, he wondered as they passed a couple of stations and bored-looking commuters piled in or drifted out. He was giddy with excitement; he fancied himself an enlightened revolutionary, a man of his word, a true champion of the republic. The romance of the moment was almost too much to bear, as was the embarrassingly mundane nature of his surroundings.

He suddenly felt inadequate. He ought to have dressed differently, symbolically, and used some other means of transport—a public bus perhaps, where, forced to rub armpits with his countrymen, he could feel even more a defender of the common interest. The cool air of the metro compartment began to feel like a knife against his cheek; the watch on his wrist a proclamation of his privilege; his tailored trousers no more cover than underpants.

He had chanced upon the Facebook post a couple of days earlier, no different than the hundreds he had ignored in the past. It was fairly simple, promising a peaceful march down one of the arterial roads of central Delhi, an apolitical one, responsible citizens making their voices heard, back home in time for dinner. Exactly the sort of dignified, responsible protest he ought to associate with. *If not now, when?*

He surveyed his co-passengers in a bid to identify more of his ilk. The shopping-laden women in front of him, busy clicking flattering pictures of themselves, were certainly not among them. The youth to his right had been a viable candidate until Roshan caught strains of the latest misogynistic Punjabi number blaring out of his earphones. His lip curled as he looked further afield.

He had not publicised it; he'd rather have that conversation after the fact. He was careful to bring it up only with people with whom he was not accustomed to having political discussions. Office colleagues made for a suitable audience. With the news blaring in the background, the previous day's lunch table had been the perfect setting.

He'd dropped it casually, as if in the habit of doing such things, and had basked in the muted, but impressed response—Priya's raised eyebrow, Akshay's brief nod of appreciation. Rashmi had even told him to be careful. Not that he was actually expecting any trouble—the event sounded far too peaceful for that—but, as his destination drew nearer, he couldn't help but feel that his safety was not guaranteed.

He was actually risking his life for something he believed in. His giddiness returned, and he lost himself in a pleasant reverie. He'd asked them, of course, if they'd like to join him, and they had said they might with an insincerity that was instantly recognisable to him.

A young girl, out of breath, flopped onto the seat to his left. Her bedraggled hair and rainbow-coloured *jhola*—no doubt purchased at a fundraiser in support of the dying arts of some forgotten tribal community—gave her away as a student. He glanced sidelong at her; catching his eye, she shot him a half-smile. Roshan looked away.

He was certain of her destination and purpose, yet could not bring himself to ask. As was usual for him in any situation bordering on the uncomfortable, he grabbed his phone and, though he had memorised the details of the venue, opened the sticky note he'd made. Perhaps she would notice and quip that she was going too.

He allowed his mind to wander. The serendipitous encounter, right before they marched down Parliament Street shoulder to shoulder, taking on the might of the Indian state together, daring to admonish it for its wrongdoings. He was disappointed to see that she had busied herself with her own phone. *No matter,* he thought. They were sure to walk out together.

Patel Chowk station. Doors will open on the right. Please mind the gap.

He rose and lingered a moment, not daring to look back. Any moment now. The doors parted, and Roshan stepped out, alone. He turned back only to see the girl grinning into her phone, her *jhola* on the seat he had just vacated.

***

Inexplicably, none of his friends had spoken of this event. Though they had stopped asking him to join others like it, someone would inevitably bring up an event or post about it on their social media. This one seemed to be Roshan's own little secret. Not that he was complaining, he thought as he stepped off the escalator.

The station looked like it might on any other day. He did not see the stream of people he had expected. As he crossed the turnstiles and began climbing the stairs leading out of the station, he heard a faint roar in the distance. Heart beating faster, the young girl forgotten, he quickened his steps.

"What a nuisance," an old man descending the steps muttered, only spurring him on. Auto-wallahs loitered near the gate, calling out their fares.

"No use, sahib," one of them said as Roshan ascended the last flight of stairs. "The road is completely blocked. But follow me to my auto and I'll take you wherever you want to go."

Roshan ignored him. The clamour was louder now. He surfaced and paused. Well, at least the number of police barricades had lived up to his expectations.

***

The crowd was a hundred, one-fifty to the generous eye. The throngs of indignant righteous that Roshan had counted himself a part of seemed to be taking their time to turn up. Slowing down, he began to walk to the barricades. Ice-cream vendors crowded nearby. Sing-song slogans, erupting from different parts of the crowd, clashed with one another.

He expected someone to stop him, to question him, but was surprised at the ease with which he slipped through. Bored-looking, *lathi*-bearing policemen swarmed around, sipping tea. The administration had deemed the threat sufficient to deploy a company of Special Forces men. They stood at the corner of the street, perspiring in the late afternoon sun, guns held flaccid at their sides. Every so often, they shot indulgent glances at the crowd, like a champion wrestler eyeing a scrawny debutant.

Beyond the barricades, a festive atmosphere prevailed on the street. People were handing out flags, pamphlets, and posters. To his utter disgust, Roshan realised that it was a political protest. The people were waving flags of the ruling party of Delhi, not one he was particularly averse to, but the apolitical, sophisticated gathering he had hoped for was not to be. His enthusiasm dimmed at once. He shifted out of the way of a party volunteer handing out pamphlets denouncing the central government.

Central Government haye haye, haye haye! Down with the Central Government!

PM, kuchh toh bolo, kuchh toh bolo! PM, speak up, speak up!

The protestors broke into little circles, the lead sloganeers' lusty yells competing with each other for attention. Gandhi caps bearing the local party symbol were visible on almost every head. Small-time pressmen mingled with the protesting crowd, taking impromptu interviews. People rushed to be part of the frame, squeezing against each other for a moment of screen time.

Roshan drifted amongst the people, moving from one small gathering to the next, unable to escape the mounting realisation that neither his presence nor his absence made any difference. The grandness of the occasion, whatever little had ever been there, was dissipating with every passing moment. Roshan felt conspicuous and invisible at the same time.

The people around him seemed to know one another, to have something to say or do. He ought to join in, to reach for a flag, feel part of it all, but he felt crippled, impotent, a nonentity in this pulsating horde.

Someone had gotten hold of a loudspeaker and was extolling the virtues of the local government, thanking its dignitaries for extending their support to this spontaneous action against the evil deeds of the Centre. The protestors cheered and resumed their chanting with renewed fervour. Someone took up a new chant.

We want justice, we want justice!

Standing close by, the man looked around for support, raising his voice with every word. He gestured at Roshan to take it up, the first person to have acknowledged him. Feeling foolish but not wanting to give offence, Roshan spoke.

"We want justice." His voice was feeble, audible only to himself. The people around him repeated the words with enthusiasm, their fists up in the air.

"We want justice," Roshan said again, trying in vain to conjure up the iconic image that had led him here, in a desperate bid to match the ardour of the crowd. He suddenly wished he had asked his friends to come or that the girl from the metro had followed him here. He imagined her safely at home, tucked away with a lover.

Beads of perspiration trickled between his shoulder blades. An energetic reporter rushed to the lead chanters, who obliged by chanting even louder and yelling about accountability and impunity at the highest levels. He could have reached out and touched their leader, but for all the proximity between them, Roshan could have been reading about him in the paper.

He wanted to speak up too, to say something, anything, but the chanting man was swallowed up by the crowd, and Roshan receded into oblivion again. He stepped onto the footpath, moving out of the way as a VIP arrived, his SUV parting the cheering crowd. He wished it were at least the chief minister—anything to make the occasion memorable, if not something to be cherished. But it was only some lowly MLA.

Roshan had drifted towards the milling Special Forces men. One of them was eating an ice-cream, the heavy gun slung over his other arm. Another made a joke to a passing protestor, and they both threw back their heads and laughed.

It would have made for a poignant moment, but all Roshan felt was anger and a hot shame—anger at this betrayal, this political carnival that had usurped his first act of direct democracy, and shame at the unmistakable conclusion that he did not belong here, could never be part of this, perhaps could not have been part of it even if it had been exactly what he had imagined.

He checked his watch. Nearly an hour had passed. His sweat-soaked t-shirt clung to him. The loudspeaker voice asked the public to move slowly and peacefully towards Parliament Street, less than a couple of hundred metres away. The crowd lurched forward; the security men near Roshan rose from their perches and sauntered after them, exuding a faint exasperation.

A passer-by in a Gandhi cap thrust a small flag at Roshan. He clutched its flimsy stick, twirling it between his forefinger and thumb. 'Justice for Victims', the caption read on one side; 'Speak up, Mr Prime Minister!' on the other. *An all-purpose flag,* he thought. Disgusted, he threw it on the road and watched it land near the police barricades.

Turning his back on the retreating crowd, Roshan stepped over the fallen flag, crossed the barricades and strode to the metro station. His first protest had lasted 58 minutes and elicited six words.

***

"Well, how was it?" Rashmi's earnest question caught him by surprise.

"How was what?" He asked, setting the salt shaker back on the table, hoping for a quick change of subject.

"Don't be modest! The protest. Tell us all about it."

Akshay, who had been discussing work with Priya in low tones, looked across. “Do tell,” he said.

Roshan’s face grew hot. He’d scoured the papers, the internet, the popular news channels for coverage of the protest, hoping not to find an incriminating image of himself, an uncomfortable, gangly outsider with an impassive face and no sense of purpose, plastered all over for the world to see. To his relief, he had found none. A lingering sense of shame had suppressed the memory of that afternoon, up till this moment, with three sets of eyes trained on him.

“It was, uh.” He cleared his throat. “It was quite something.”

No employee had ever yearned for a work call quite as much as he at that moment.

“What do you mean? Come on, don’t be shy. We told you on Friday that we’ve never done this kind of thing before,” Priya said.

And I still haven’t, Roshan thought to himself.

“Sorry, Roshan, I hope it’s not difficult to talk about,” Rashmi said.

“No, it’s not like that. Maybe it is, a bit,” he heard himself say.

“It was—glorious. I’ve never seen a crowd like that in my life. People as far as the eye could see. The Centre had to send three units of Special Forces to contain them. Us.”

“What was it like?” Akshay sounded doubtful.

“Simply marvellous! Thousands of people coming together in a spontaneous expression of compassion and power; it was a heady feeling. The plan was to march, but the response was so overwhelming and the number so large that we occupied the entire road, end to end. We didn’t need to march. The police were trying to stir up trouble, taunting us, provoking us. But the crowd was undaunted. It was meant to be a peaceful protest and stayed as such. A peaceful protest in the highest traditions of Indian democracy.”

“Such a large protest and no media coverage?”

"Surely, Priya," Roshan said, turning to her, "you don't believe everything you read? The fourth estate has sold out to the highest bidder. They would never cover us. Ten seconds of footage would show the protest, the movement, for the awe-inspiring success it was. The government could never allow that to come to pass."

"Makes sense," Akshay said. "Yet—"

"Leave him alone!" Rashmi cried. "The man risked his neck, for heaven's sake—you know what they do to brave journalists and the like these days, don't you? A little less scepticism would be nice. Do go on, Roshan," she finished, flashing him a charming little smile.

Their conversation had piqued the curiosity of a couple of their other colleagues, including some from other departments whom Roshan didn't know. They pulled their chairs around.

"I wouldn't have gone in the ordinary course, you know," he continued, pausing to take a sip of water. "But what happened at Thoothukudi, it was—"

"Unpardonable," supplied a youth with a goatee, who looked like he was fresh out of college. Roshan rewarded him with an appreciative look.

"Unpardonable," Roshan repeated. "A vile act! I just couldn't sit still. If not now, when?"

A few in his audience nodded, looking solemn.

"I have always held the Indian state in high regard. But sometimes, you just need to point your leaders in the right direction. And only the popular will works when it comes to this kind of thing."

"Wah!" The HR manager said from the corner. "It's wonderful to see young people like you, with such busy jobs to boot, getting involved in something like this. Really inspiring."

"When we got there, there were only khaki policemen," Roshan said, cutting him off. "With lathis. They didn't frighten us, so they did their best with their taunts and jibes, calling us—"

"What, what did they say?" Goatee's friend asked. Roshan rested his eyes on her, taking in the scene. A few others, including—his heart skipped a beat—the CEO had taken their seats at nearby tables. He could tell that they were keeping an ear out for his response. The TV blared on, forgotten, in the background.

"Liberal whores," he said, to a collective intake of breath. "Sell-outs. Bastard children of immoral, unpatriotic JNU graduates. Said that those people deserved what they got for spreading lies about the factory and not behaving themselves."

"And?" Priya asked.

"And that we'd get the same if we didn't toe the line and go home. A couple of them had revolvers and brandished them at us, saying they were authorised to use them if they deemed fit."

There was shocked silence.

"It's only natural that the government wouldn't want you to hear all this, you know. I'd request you to keep it all to yourself," Roshan said, shooting a beseeching look at Rashmi.

This was greeted by murmurs of 'of course' and 'never' and even 'damn the police, corrupt, servile thugs'.

"These goons didn't frighten us. Some of the crowd even talked back and got knocks on their heads. So did I, of course, but I managed to escape; I got lucky. It was only when the Special Forces rolled up in their armoured car, parting the crowds—I was scared then, I won't deny it."

"Who wouldn't be?" Someone from the CEO's table quipped. "They're equipped with proper assault weapons, aren't they?"

"The very best," Roshan agreed. "It was a daunting sight. They lined the road, trying to intimidate us, push us in, make us beat a retreat. But the crowd was marvellous. Nobody knew who was in charge, yet everyone stuck to their positions, held up their banners, and put on a good, peaceful show. Of course—" he shovelled in a mouthful of rice, and took his time to chew. Nobody moved from their places.

"Of course, a couple of opposition leaders showed up to show solidarity towards the end."

"Slimy fuckers."

"They should've been the ones organising the protest."

"The movement. And yes, they should have," Roshan said, taking another thoughtful bite. "Needless to say, we made it clear that they were not welcome. Even the forces did nothing to help them, forgetting that they were their masters not too long ago. They had to scarper soon, or face the full wrath of the people."

Someone whooped.

"The best part, though," Roshan continued, "was the discipline of it all. It was an audacious, idealistic gathering. Yet, it was made up of like-minded individuals. There was none of the chest-thumping of the past. People came at the appointed hour, behaved themselves, made their point, and left when asked to disperse."

"So, you just left?" Akshay asked. "Such a large movement of people, and it didn't cause any chaos?"

"Well, Akshay, the police had been kind enough to cordon off the area," Roshan said, flashing him a withering look. "And like I said, the crowd was so orderly, it was amazing to see. I myself simply walked back to the metro station and came home. The compartment was full of people from the protest—we didn't know one another, we didn't even speak much, yet we felt an indescribable solidarity, an empathy born of our common experience."

"What did you do then?" A pretty girl from accounts, whose name he could not remember, asked. "What did you do after getting home on Saturday night, the whole of Sunday? How did it feel?"

Roshan smiled. "I can't say. I was in a bit of a daze. Came home and slept. Scoured the news for coverage all of Sunday, even the petty channels and papers, but there was nothing. As expected," he finished with a heavy sigh.

"Hey, there's something on about the Thoothukudi matter now!" Someone near the TV said. Heads turned away from Roshan for the first time in nearly an hour.

Roshan stared straight ahead, his mouth dry.

This is just in. The Prime Minister has finally broken his silence on what he terms the 'horrific' police action in Thoothukudi. All officials involved in the action stand suspended pending an independent probe into the matter. The factory in question has been sealed for the time being. The opposition is already claiming this as its victory, attributing the PM's orders to its incessant criticism.

Heads turned back to him.

"You won, man," Goatee said. A moment later, the cafeteria broke into spontaneous applause. Akshay reached out to thump Roshan on the back. They stopped when the CEO cleared his throat and walked up to their table. Roshan rose, unsteady on his feet.

"It is because of people like you, *beta*," the CEO said, "that our democracy survives, and thrives. Thank you." He reached out and gave Roshan's clammy hand a vigorous, solemn shake.

Ignoring the memory of the paunchy, detached Special Forces officer enjoying his Mother Dairy ice lolly, Roshan replied, looking the CEO straight in the eye, "You're very welcome, Sir."

•

Living

His eyes flicker open, a peaceful smile tugging at the corners of his lips. He tends to rise like this these days. It is new. Ma, Pa, and then Amu always complained that he wore a frown first thing, however pleasant the close of the previous day.

Sometimes, they meld together in his dreams and mind's eye, chiding and coddling him by turn, in unison. He often tries to prise them apart, but soon gives up, exhausted by the effort. After all, he could dream of worse things than the three most precious beings to him fusing into one.

Daybreak is still distant. Another new trend. *Trend.* He allows the smile to fill out and chuckles. The word hardly fits. He was never an early riser. Sometimes, he marvels at the sheer fact of his having spent so many years just *doing* things that required him to get out of bed at a reasonable hour.

"Not today, friend," he whispers, offering thanks for seeing another day. He sits up slowly, shivering at the slight nip in the air as he eases his legs off the bed. It is just September, but this is as sure a sign as any that winter is on the way. Bringing with it the grey, throttling fog that grips the frigid city in a malevolent embrace for what always seems like more weeks than the last year. It is harder to bear each time.

He could move, but wouldn't know where to. He has never known anything but this city. A life well-spent, a life well-spent. He imagines this is what people might say once he melts away, commenting in polite tones on his unobtrusive nature, his quiet ways, and small smiles in his last years. And isn't it?

His reflection eyes him coolly from the mirror, observing his bony wrist work the razor on his face. A non-critical stare. A novelty. Discovered almost too late.

The faint light and warmth of the day begin to trickle through as he concludes his routine. It is quick now, his frugal intake not always necessitating an output. Shutting the door on the toilet, he shrugs. As long as he feels good.

He moves to the living room. There is nothing to do, nowhere to go, nobody to meet. He sinks into an armchair, emitting a low groan as it swallows up his thin frame. He has some friends, of course. They all talk of the same things. Children. Medicines. Retirement expenses. Grandchildren.

They tend to exude positivity and peace, none speaking of their old lives with regret, or much at all, in fact. As if to say, without speaking, that that chapter is well over. We liberated ourselves from it long ago. It is different for him. Or so he feels. Sometimes, he really wonders what they *think* to themselves alone, in their quiet moments. Surely there is little to really think about other than the life lived.

It always occupies his thoughts. But he cannot pin it down. He feels giddy, like after his first cigarette, trying to bring all those thoughts, all those memories, to heel. He can only see glimpses of frenetic activity and colour; swift, blinding, marvellous. The life well-lived.

It is always only one thing that is clear. He stretches his legs out and places them on the ottoman with a sigh, unable to redirect his stream of consciousness. It is so distant, like a virulent childhood flu; yet so intimate, like a piece of skin.

There has to be something more. Fresh as ever, the words gnaw at his heart. He spoke them aloud even when he knew they hurt others, the very ones who felt that they filled up his life, repeated the words even when he knew they caused unwarranted resentment in him towards a life most would envy.

Thought them with increasing frequency as the letters of rejection kept rolling in. Ever pert, ever polite, ever unmoved by his hours of toil, both at the office desk and the writing desk. The numbers of the few which bore a line or two of encouragement, a regularity at the outset, dwindled steadily.

This just wasn't part of the plan. He chuckles, the second time the same morning. *The plan.* The very concept, so addictive, tenacious, all-consuming, is jarring in this new world he inhabits. One in which every moment of every day seems to stretch on endlessly, neither with nor without promise.

He shuffles over to his writing desk and drops into the ancient high-backed chair Amu had bought him. His computer hums in the corner. Yesterday was a paper day. Loose leaves are strewn about, covered in his now-spidery print. He ought to gather them and make sense of the previous evening's work, but he lets them be for the moment.

Sometimes he flew into a rage, deleted or tore up whatever he could get his hands on, railing against his own mediocrity, his inability to achieve a goal none had thrust upon him; to break free, to stand miles apart living the extraordinary life, to have the last of the laughs. Or he would abandon the last vestiges of hope and weep like a baby, clutching Amu's breast.

He shuts his eyes, breathes in, then out. Did it ever have to be so difficult? They were comfortable, lacked nothing. He sometimes allowed himself to reflect on this during those bitter years of silence when he had let his writing desk gather dust, not letting even Amu touch it.

Just enough to reach the precipice of the truth, but never enough to tip himself over. No. What was the purpose of art if it could not become his ticket out? And so, the silence, destined to be broken only by a fairy-tale success still fantasised about, but long since given up on, stretched on.

Pa passed on, then Ma. He clung to Amu as tight as he could, compelled their life together to trundle along as far as he could beg it to. But too soon, it was her time too. Even as she passed, she seemed to know exactly what he needed. The first time after her, more than a year after, when he absently found himself at this exact spot and rifled through the drawers of his writing desk, he spotted them.

His manuscripts, stacked in a neat pile by her loving hands, patiently awaited discovery. Despite himself, he devoured them like words emerged from a foreign hand. The unread, undiscovered, unappreciated words flowed through his soul like music. And the bitter silence slipped away. The house heard once more the scratches of his pen and the taps of his keyboard.

This could be me. Should be. He uttered these words in each bookstore he and Amu happened to visit, glaring at the loud imprints of the many he considered foolish but lucky. If he happened to chance upon any works of a contemporary, someone he had known, submitted to, or corresponded with, the offending bookstore had to lose their patronage.

He glances at the paperback on the desk, delivered just yesterday. The latest work of an editor at whose hands he had suffered no less than ten rejections. Looking away from the book, he smiles at Amu's dimpled grin in the frame before him. He used to talk to her earlier, addressing her many portraits within the house. But words seem unnecessary now.

He sighs again. The days are rolling by, pleasant and unhurried. Time, his adversary, if not enemy, for all but this last stub of life, now seems to pause by him like a curious friend. A son, friend, lover, worker, husband. What else, nothing more?

He shakes his head at himself, willing these thoughts to recede, and at the bubbling blurb screaming out of the cover of the editor's book. Should it be him? Probably. His eyes rest on the bookshelf to his right, covered now with his manuscripts, stories, notes, and poems.

Could it be him? He doesn't know. Nobody has read his work in seventeen years. And yet, he writes. So, isn't there something more? Isn't it a part of the plan? He doesn't know. It doesn't matter.

Smiling, he reaches out for a blank loose-leaf, unscrews his pen, nods at Amu, and begins to write. A life well-spent.

Notes on a Few Stories

Skin

This story originally appeared in Guftugu (January 2019).

The Perfect Cut

I must clarify that this story can be read as auto-fiction only to the extent of my personal struggles with maths at the higher levels (a standing joke amongst my close friends). I've been fortunate to always have the staunch love and support of my family in whatever I've chosen to do (and perhaps more important – what I've chosen not *to do).*

The Bet

Needless to say, this story was written before 24 October 2021. But then, we still have the *World Cup (and based on recent relative skill levels and performance – everything else too!)*

Bravado

This story originally appeared in Kitaab (March 2019).

Acknowledgements

Foremost – a big thank you to Ritika, my first reader, end-to-end advisor through the entire process of bringing this book to fruition, and all too often, co-brooder about the state and prospects of my writing. Your belief that this is meaningful work which I ought not to give up on, and that I am going about it the right way, irrespective of outcomes, means the world.

Thanks to my friend Ranjini, who read this manuscript long before it was officially submitted, and gave me several helpful insights (not least that I had unwittingly used the expression "Brownian motion" more than once!).

Thanks to Suhail Mathur and his team at *The Book Bakers (TBB)*, my literary agent, for believing in this book and his timely and helpful guidance and inputs throughout the pitching process and thereafter.

Thanks to the boys of Fakland for always cheering me on. It is the one place which regularly acknowledges me as a writer, sometimes jokingly and sometimes otherwise, but each time, it means something to me!

Many thanks to the team at *Srishti* for taking a chance on this book, for their thorough work on the manuscript, and their constant support and guidance in bringing this to market.

Finally – thank you to the many other friends, relatives, acquaintances, and most importantly – strangers – who have read things I've written. You are perhaps too many to name, but always in my thoughts. I hope this book finds its way to you!